Also available in Large Print
by Rex Stout:

The Broken Vase
The Mother Hunt

A Nero Wolfe Mystery
Prisoner's Base

Rex Stout

G.K.HALL & CO.
Boston, Massachusetts
1988

Published in Large Print by arrangement with
Barbara Stout and Rebecca Stout Bradbury.

G.K. Hall Large Print Book Series.

Set in 16 pt Plantin.

Library of Congress Cataloging in Publication Data

Stout, Rex, 1886-1975.
  Prisoner's base : a Nero Wolfe mystery / Rex Stout.
    p.   cm.—(G.K. Hall large print book series)
  (Nightingale series)
  ISBN 0-8161-4391-9
  1. Large type books. I. Title.
PS3537.T733P75 1988
813'.52—dc19   88-16284

Prisoner's Base

In Nero Wolfe's old brownstone house on West Thirty-fifth Street that Monday afternoon in June, the atmosphere was sparky. I mention it not to make an issue of Wolfe's bad habits, but because it is to the point. It was the atmosphere that got us a roomer.

What had stirred it up was a comment made by Wolfe three days earlier. Each Friday morning at eleven, when he comes down to the office on the first floor from the plant rooms on the roof, Wolfe signs the salary checks for Fritz and Theodore and me, hands me mine, and keeps the other two because he likes to deliver them personally. That morning, as he passed mine across his desk, he made a remark.

"Thank you for waiting for it."

My brows went up. "What's the matter? Bugs on the orchids?"

"No. But I saw your bag in the hall, and I note your finery. Straining as you are to be gone, it is gracious of you to wait for this pittance, this meager return for your excessive labors in the week nearly ended. Especially since the bank balance is at its lowest point in two years."

I controlled myself. "That deserves an answer, and here it is. As for finery, I am headed for a weekend in the country and am dressed accordingly. As for straining, I am not." I glanced at my wrist. "I have ample time to get the car and drive to Sixty-third Street to get Miss Rowan. As for pittance, right. As for excessive labors, I have had to spend most of my time recently sitting on my prat only because you have seen fit to turn down four offers of jobs in a row. As for the week nearly ended, meaning that I am dashing off to carouse before the week is out for which I am being paid, you've known about it for a month, and what's here to keep me? As for the bank balance, there I admit you have a point. I'm the bookkeeper and I know, and I'm willing to help. It's only a pittance anyway, what the hell."

I took my check, with thumbs and forefingers at the middle of its top edge, tore it across, put the halves together and tore again, dropped the shreds into my wastebasket, and turned and started for the door. His bellow came at me.

"Archie!"

I wheeled and glared at him. He glared back. "Pfui," he said.

"Nuts," I said, and turned and went.

That was what created the atmosphere. When I returned from the country late Sunday night he had gone up to bed. By Monday morning the air might possibly have cleared if it hadn't been for the torn-up check. We both knew the stub would have to be voided and a new check drawn, but he wasn't going to tell me to do it without being asked, and I wasn't going to do it without being told. A man has his pride. With that between us, the stiffness Monday morning lasted through lunch and beyond, into the afternoon.

Around 4:30 I was at my desk, working on the germination records, when the doorbell rang. Ordinarily, unless instructions have been given, Fritz answers it, but that day my legs needed stretching and I went. Swinging the door open, I took in a sight that led me to an agreeable conclusion. The suitcase and hatbox could have held a salesman's samples, but the young woman in the light peach-colored dress and tailored jacket was surely no peddler. Calling on Nero Wolfe with luggage, ten to one she was a prospective client from out of town, and, coming straight from the station or airport, in a hurry. Such a one was welcome.

With the hatbox dangling from her hand, she crossed the threshold, brushed past me, and said, "You're Archie Goodwin. Will you bring my suitcase in? Please?"

I did so, closed the door, and deposited the suitcase against the wall. She put the hatbox down beside it and straightened to speak.

"I want to see Nero Wolfe, but of course he's always up in the plant rooms from four to six. That's why I picked this time to come, I want to see you first." Her eyes moved. "That's the door to the front room." Her eyes moved again, aimed the length of the hall. "That's the stairs, and the door to the dining room on the right and to the office on the left. The hall's wider than I expected. Shall we go to the office?"

I had never seen eyes like hers. Either they were brownish gray flecked with brownish yellow, or brownish yellow flecked with brownish gray. They were deep in, wide apart, and moved fast.

4

"What's the matter?" she asked.

That was phony. She must have been used to people, at first sight of those eyes, staring at them; she probably expected it. I told her nothing was the matter, took her to the office, and gave her a chair, sat at my desk, and observed, "So you've been here before."

She shook her head. "A friend of mine was here a long while ago, and then of course I've read about it." She looked around, twisting her head to the right and then to the left. "I wouldn't have come if I hadn't known a good deal about it, and about Nero Wolfe and you." She leveled the eyes at me, and, finding it difficult to meet them casually, I met them consciously. She went on, "I thought it would be better to tell you about it first because I'm not sure I would know how to put it to Nero Wolfe. You see, I'm trying to work something out. I wonder—do you know what I think I need right now?"

"No. What?"

"A Coke and rum with some lime and lots of ice. I don't suppose you've got Meyer's?"

It seemed to me she was crowding a little, but I said sure, we had everything, and got up to step to Wolfe's desk and ring for Fritz. When he had come and got the order, and I was back in my chair, she spoke again. "Fritz looks younger than I expected," she said.

I leaned back and clasped my hands behind my head. "You're welcome to a drink, even a Coke and rum," I told her, "and I'm enjoying your company, that's okay, but if you want me to tell you how to put something to Mr. Wolfe maybe you'd better start."

"Not till I've had the drink," she said firmly.

She not only had the drink, she made herself at home. After Fritz had brought it and she had taken a couple of sips, she murmured something about its being warm and removed the jacket and dropped it on the seat of the red leather chair. Furthermore, she took off the straw thing she had on her head, fingered her hair back, and got a mirror from her bag and gave herself a brief look. Then, with her glass in her hand, and sipping intermittently, she moved to my desk for a glance at the germination cards, crossed to the big globe and gave it a gentle spin, and went to the shelves and looked at titles of books. When her glass

6

was empty she put it on a table, went to her chair and sat, and gave me the eyes.

"I'm beginning to get myself together," she told me.

"Good. Don't rush it."

"I won't. I'm not a rusher. I'm a very cautious girl—believe me, I am. I never rushed but one thing in my life, and that one was enough. I'm not sure I'm over it yet. I think maybe I should have another drink."

I decided against it. I couldn't deny that the effect Coke and rum had on her was pleasant; it tuned her up and emphasized her charms, which were fair enough without the emphasis. But this was office hours, and I wanted to find out if she had any potential as a client. So I decided to dodge the drink problem with a polite suggestion, but before I had it framed she demanded, "Does the door of the south room on the third floor have a bolt on the inside?"

I frowned at her. I was beginning to suspect she was something we couldn't use, like for instance a female writer getting material for a magazine piece on a famous detective's home, but even so she was not the kind to be led out by the ear and rolled off the stoop down the steps to the sidewalk.

7

There was no good reason, considering the eyes, why she shouldn't be humored up to a point.

"No," I said. "Why, do you think it needs one?"

"Maybe not," she conceded, "but I thought I'd feel better if it had. You see, that's where I want to sleep."

"Oh? You do? For about how long?"

"For a week. Possibly a day or two more, but certainly for a week. I would rather have the south room than the one on the second floor because it has its own bath. I know how Nero Wolfe feels about women, so I knew I'd have to see you first."

"That was sensible," I agreed. "I like gags, and I'll bet this is a pip. How does it go?"

"It is not a gag." She wasn't heated, but she was earnest. "For a certain reason I had to be—I had to go away. I had to go somewhere and stay there until June thirtieth—some place where no one would know and no one could possibly find me. I didn't think a hotel would do, and I didn't think—anyhow, I thought it over and decided the best place would be Nero Wolfe's house. Nobody knows I came; nobody followed me here, I'm sure of that."

8

She got up and went to the red leather chair for her bag, which she had left there with her jacket. Back in her seat, she opened the bag and took out a purse and let me have the eyes again. "One thing you can tell me," she said, as if I not only could but naturally would, "—about paying. I know how he charges just for wiggling his finger. Would it be better for me to offer to pay him or to go ahead and pay you now? Would fifty dollars a day be enough? Whatever you say. I'll give you cash instead of a check, because that way he won't have to pay income tax on it, and also because a check would have my name on it, and I don't want you to know my name. I'll give it to you now if you'll tell me how much."

"That won't do," I objected. "Hotels and rooming houses have to know names. We can make one up for you. How would Lizzie Borden do?"

She reacted to that crack as she had to the Coke and rum—she flushed a little. "You think it's funny?" she inquired.

I was firm. "So far," I declared, "the over-all effect is comical. You aren't going to tell us your name?"

"No."

"Or where you live? Anything at all?"

"No."

"Have you committed a crime or been accessory to one? Are you a fugitive from justice?"

"No."

"Prove it."

"That's silly! I don't have to prove it!"

"You do if you expect to get bed and board here. We're particular. Altogether four murderers have slept in the south room—the last one was a Mrs. Floyd Whitten, some three years ago. And I am personally interested, since that room is on the same floor as mine." I shook my head regretfully. "Under the circumstances, there's no point in continuing the chinning, which is a pity, since I have nothing special to do and you are by no means a scarecrow, but unless you see fit to open up—"

I stopped short because it suddenly struck me that in any case I could do better than shoo her out. Even if she couldn't be cast as a client, I could still use her.

I looked at her. "I don't know," I said doubtfully. "Tell me your name."

"No," she said positively.

"Why not?"

"Because—what good would it do unless you checked on it? How would you know it was my real name? And I don't want you checking on it. I don't want anyone to have the faintest idea where I am for a week—until June thirtieth."

"What happens on June thirtieth?"

She shook her head, smiling at me. "You're good at asking questions, I know that, so I'm not going to answer any at all. I don't want you to do anything, or Nero Wolfe either, except to let me stay here for a week, right in that room, for my meals too. I think I've already talked too much. I think I should have said—no, I guess that wouldn't have worked." She laughed a little, a low running ripple. "If I had said I had read about you and seen a picture of you, and you fascinated me, and I wanted to be near you for one wonderful week, you'd have known I was lying."

"Not necessarily. Millions of women feel like that, but they can't afford the fifty bucks a day."

"I said I would pay more. Whatever you say."

"Yeah, I know. Let's get this settled. Are you going to stick to this—no naming or identifying?"

"I certainly intend to."

"Then you'd better leave Mr. Wolfe to

11

me." I glanced at my wrist. "He'll be coming down in three-quarters of an hour." I left my chair. "I'll take you up and leave you there, and when he comes down I'll tackle him. With no tag on you it's probably hopeless, but I may be able to persuade him to listen to you." I picked up her jacket and turned. "It might help if he saw the cash. Sometimes the sight of money has an effect on people. Say three hundred and fifty, as you suggested? With the understanding, of course, that it's not a deal until Mr. Wolfe accepts it."

Her fingers were quick and accurate as they ticked off seven new fifties from the stack she got from her purse. She had enough left. I stuck our share in my pocket, went to the hall for the suitcase and hatbox, and led the way up the stairs, two flights. The door to the south room was standing open. Inside I put the luggage down, went and pulled the cords of the venetian blinds for light, and cranked a window open.

She stood, taking a look around. "It's a big room," she said approvingly. She lifted a hand as if to touch my sleeve, but let it drop. "I appreciate this, Mr. Goodwin."

I grunted. I was not prepared to get on terms with her. Putting the suitcase on the rack at the foot of one of the twin beds, and the hatbox on a chair, I told her, "I'll have to watch you unpack these."

Her eyes widened. "Watch me? Why?"

"For the kick." I was slightly exasperated. "There are at least a thousand people in the metropolitan area who think Nero Wolfe has lived long enough, and one or more of them might have decided to take a hand. His room, as you apparently know, is directly below this. What I expect to find is a brace and bit in the suitcase and a copperhead or rattler in the hatbox. Are they locked?"

She regarded me to see if I was kidding, decided I wasn't, and stepped over and opened the suitcase. I was right there. On top was a blue silk negligee, which she lifted and put on the bed.

"For the kick," she said indignantly.

"It hurts me worse than it does you," I assured her. "Just pretend I'm not here."

I'm not a lingerie expert, but I know what I like, and that was quite a collection. There was one plain white folded garment, sheer as gossamer, with the finest mesh I had ever seen. As she put it on the bed I asked politely, "Is that a blouse?"

"No. Pajama."

13

"Oh. Excellent for hot weather."

When everything was out of the suitcase I picked it up for a good look, pressing with my fingertips on the sides and ends, inside and out. I wasn't piling it on; among the unwanted articles that had been introduced into that house in some sort of container were a fer-de-lance, a tear-gas bomb, and a cylinder of cyanogen. But there was nothing tricky about the construction of the suitcase, or the hatbox either; and as for the contents, you couldn't ask for a prettier or completer display of the personal requirements of a young woman for a quiet and innocent week in a private room of the house of a private detective.

I backed off. "I guess that'll do," I granted. "I haven't inspected your handbag, nor your person, so I hope you won't mind if I lock the door. If you sneaked down to Mr. Wolfe's room and put a cyanide pill in his aspirin bottle, and he took it and died, I'd be out of a job."

"Certainly." She hissed it. "Lock it good. That's the kind of thing I do every day."

"Then you need a caretaker, and I'm it. How about a drink?"

"If it isn't too much bother."

I said it wasn't and left her, locking the

14

door with the key I had brought along from the office. Downstairs, after stopping in the kitchen to tell Fritz we had a guest locked in the south room, to ask him to take her up a drink, and to give him the key, I went to the office, took the seven fifties from my pocket, worked them into a fan, and put them under a paperweight on Wolfe's desk.

—2————————————————————

At one minute past six, when the sound came of Wolfe's elevator descending, I got so busy with things on my desk that I didn't have time to turn my head when he entered the office. I followed him by ear—crossing to his chair behind his desk, getting his four thousand ounces seated and adjusted in comfort, ringing for beer, grunting as he reached for the book he was reading, left there by him two hours earlier, his place marked by a counterfeit ten-dollar bill which had been autographed in red ink by a former Secretary of the Treasury in appreciation of services rendered. I also caught, by ear, Wolfe speaking to Fritz when he brought the beer.

"Did you put this money here, Fritz?"

15

Of course that forced me. I swiveled. "No, sir, I did."

"Indeed. Thank you, Fritz." He got his eighteen-carat opener from the drawer, uncapped a bottle, and poured. Fritz departed. Wolfe let the foam subside a little, not too much, lifted the glass, and took two healthy swallows. Putting the glass down, he tapped the new non-counterfeit fifties, still in a fan under the paperweight, with a fingertip, and demanded, "Well? Flummery?"

"No, sir."

"Then what?"

I bubbled with eager frankness. "I admit it, sir, what you said Friday about my excessive labors and the bank balance—that really hurt. I felt I wasn't doing my share, with you sweating it out four hours a day up with the orchids. I was sitting here this afternoon mulling over it, some of the hardest mulling I've ever done, when the doorbell rang."

He was reacting to my opening as expected. Turning to his place in the book, he started reading. I went right on.

"It was a human female in her twenties, with unprecedented eyes, a fine wholesome figure, a highly polished leather suitcase, and a hatbox. She tooted her knowledge of the premises and you and me, bragging about her reading. I brought her in here and we chatted. She wouldn't tell her name or anything else about herself. She wants no advice, no information, no detective work, no nothing. All she wants is board and room for one week, with meals served in her room, and she specified the south room, which, as you know, is on the same floor as mine."

I made a little gesture signifying modesty. With his eyes on the book, he didn't see it, but I made it anyway. "With your trained mind, naturally you have already reached the conclusion that I was myself compelled to accept, on the evidence. Not only has she read about me, she has seen my picture, and she can't stand it not to be near me—as she put it, for one wonderful week. Luckily she is supplied with lettuce, and she paid for the week in advance, at fifty bucks a day. That's where that came from. I told her I was taking it only tentatively, awaiting your okay, and took her up to the south room and helped her unpack, and locked her in. She's there now."

He had turned in his chair for better light on his book, practically turning his back on me. I went on, unruffled. "She said some-

17

thing about having to go somewhere and stay until June thirtieth, where no one could find her, but of course she had to put some kind of face on it. I made no personal commitments, but I won't object to some sacrifice of time and convenience, provided I average eight hours' sleep. She seems educated and refined and will probably want me to read aloud to her, so I'll have to ask you to lend me some books, like *Pilgrim's Progress* and *Essays of Elia*. She also seems sweet and unspoiled and has fine legs, so if we like her and get used to her one of us could marry her. However, the immediate point is that, since I am responsible for that handy little contribution of cash, you may feel like signing a replacement for the check I tore up Friday."

I got it from a drawer, where I had it ready, and got up to put it on his desk. He put his book down, took his pen from the stand, signed the check, and slid it across to me.

He regarded me with what looked like amiable appreciation. "Archie," he told me, "that was an impressive performance. Friday I spoke hastily and you acted hastily, and the *fait accompli* of that torn check had us at an impasse. It was an awkward problem, and you have solved it admirably. By contriving one of your fantastically and characteristically puerile inventions, you made the problem itself absurd and so disposed of it. Admirable and satisfactory."

He removed the paperweight from the fifties, picked them up, jiggled the edges even, and extended his hand with them, telling me, "I didn't know we had fifties in the emergency cash reserve. Better put them back. I don't like money lying around."

I didn't take the dough. "Hold it," I said. "We're bumping."

"Bumping?"

"Yes, sir. That didn't come from the safe. It came from a visitor as described, now up in the south room. I invented nothing, puerile or not. She's a roomer for a week if you want her. Shall I bring her down so you can decide?"

He was glaring at me. "Bah," he said, reaching for his book.

"Okay, I'll go get her." I started for the door, expecting him to stop me with a roar, but he didn't. He thought he knew I was playing him. I compromised by going to the kitchen to ask Fritz to come in a minute, and let him precede me back to the office. Wolfe didn't glance at us.

"A little point of information," I told Fritz. "Mr. Wolfe thinks I'm exaggerating. Our lady visitor you took a drink to up in the south room—is she old, haggard, deformed, ugly, and crippled."

"Now, Archie," Fritz reproved me. "She is quite the opposite. Precisely the opposite."

"Right. You left her locked in?"

"Certainly. I brought you the key. You said she would probably have her dinner—"

"Yeah, we'll let you know. Okay, thanks."

Fritz darted a look at Wolfe, got none in return, wheeled, and left. Wolfe waited for the sound of the kitchen door closing, then put his book down and spoke. "It's true," he said in a tone that would have been fitting if he had just learned that I had been putting thrips on his plants. "You have actually installed a woman in a room of my house?"

"Not installed exactly," I objected. "That's too strong a word. And it implies that I have personal—"

"Where did you get her?"

"I didn't get her. As I told you, she came. I wasn't inventing. I was reporting."

"Report it in full. Verbatim."

20

That order was easy, compared to some I have had to fill. I gave him words and actions complete, from opening the front door to let her in through to locking the south room door to keep her in. He leaned back with his eyes closed, as he usually does when I'm reporting at length. When I finished he had no questions, not one. He merely opened his eyes and snapped at me, "Go up and give her back her money." He glanced at the wall clock. "It'll be dinnertime in twenty minutes. Get her out of the house in ten. Help her pack."

Here I hit a snag. Looking back at it, it would seem that my natural and normal course would have been to obey instructions. My double mission had been accomplished. I had taken a backhanded crack at his being so damn particular about accepting jobs and clients, and also I had got a replacement for my check. She had served my purpose, so why not bounce her? But evidently something about her, maybe the way she packed a suitcase, had made an impression on me, for I found myself taking a line.

I told Wolfe that, acting as his agent, I had practically promised her that he would see her. He only grunted. I told him that he could probably get her to can the mystery and tell her name and describe her troubles, and if so the resulting fee might provide for my salary checks for a year. Another grunt.

I gave up. "Okay," I said, "she'll have to find some bacalhau somewhere else. Maybe East Harlem—there's a lot of Portuguese around there. I shouldn't have mentioned it to her."

"Bacalhau?" he demanded.

"Yeah. I happened to mention we were having it for dinner, and she asked what it was and I told her, and she said salt cod couldn't possibly be fit to eat no matter how it was cooked, not even if it was an adaptation of a Portuguese recipe by you and Fritz." I shrugged. "Skip it. She may be a murderess anyhow. What's the difference if we break a precedent by turning her out hungry just at mealtime? What if I did sell her on salt cod and now have to evict her unfed? Who am I?"

I got up and picked up the seven fifties from his desk. "This," I said regretfully, "puts us back where we started. Since this is to be returned to her, I have contributed nothing to the bank account, and the situation regarding my salary check snaps back to last Friday. That leaves me no alternative." I reached to my desk for the check he had signed as replacement, took it at the middle of its top edge with thumbs and forefingers—

"Archie!" he roared. "Don't tear that!"

I still do not know what the decision would have been about the roomer upstairs if it had been left to us. Because Wolfe did not like the idea of sending anyone from his house hungry, because of his instinctive reaction to the challenge that salt cod couldn't be made edible, and because of my threat to tear up another check, the roomer was not bounced before dinner, and the tray that was prepared for the south room was inspected personally by Wolfe before Fritz took it up. But except for the preparation and dispatch of the tray, no decision was put into words; the question was ignored. Wolfe and I ate together in the dining room as usual; the salt cod with Portuguese trimmings was so good that I had no room for the veal and not much for the walnut pudding; and when we were through with coffee and I followed Wolfe back into the office I assumed that the first item on the agenda would be Miss or Mrs. X. But he didn't even call a meeting. After a full meal, which our dinner always is, it takes him four or five minutes to get adjusted in his chair to his complete satisfaction. With that accomplished that Monday evening, he opened his book and started to read.

I had nothing to complain about, since it was certainly his move. She was still up there, fed and locked in, and it was up to him. He could just pass it and let her stay, which was unthinkable, or he could have me bring her down for a talk, which he would hate, or he could tell me to put her out, which might or might not get my prompt cooperation. In any case, I didn't intend to give him an opening, so when he started reading I sat regarding him silently for a couple of minutes and then got up and headed for the door.

His voice came at me from behind. "You're not going out?"

I turned and was bland. "Why not?"

"That woman you smuggled in. The arrangement was that you would get rid of her after dinner."

It was a barefaced lie; there had been no such arrangement, and he knew it. But he had unquestionably squared off and feinted with a jab, and it was my turn. The disposal of our roomer would probably have been settled quickly and finally if it hadn't been

24

for an interruption. The doorbell rang. It was only two steps from where I stood to the hall, and I took them.

After dark I never open the outside door to a ring without first flipping on the stoop light and taking a look through the one-way panel. That time a glance was enough. He was alone, about twice my age, tall and bony with a square jutting jaw, with a dark gray felt hat firmly on his head and a brief-case under his arm. I pulled the door open and asked him how he did. Ignoring that question, he said his name was Perry Helmar and that he wanted to see Nero Wolfe, urgently. Ordinarily, when Wolfe is in the office and a stranger calls, I let the caller wait while I go in to check, but now, welcoming a chance to give Wolfe another tack to sit on, and also perhaps to postpone a showdown on the roomer until bedtime, I invited the guy in, hung his hat on the rack, and escorted him to the office.

I thought for a second that Wolfe was going to get up and march out without a word. I have known him to do that more than once, upon deciding that someone, not always me, is not to be borne. The idea did dart into his mind—I know that look only too well—but it wasn't strong enough to overcome his reluctance to leave his chair. So he sat and surveyed the visitor with a resentful scowl.

"I should explain," Helmar explained, "that I came to you immediately not only because I know something of your record and reputation, but also because I know my friend Dick Williamson's opinion of you— Richard A. Williamson, the cotton broker. He says you once performed a miracle for him."

Helmar paused politely to give Wolfe a chance to insert an acknowledgment of this flattering preamble. Wolfe did so by inclining his head a full eighth of an inch.

"I don't ask for a miracle," Helmar resumed, "but I do need speed, boldness, and sagacity." He was in the red leather chair beyond the end of Wolfe's desk, with his briefcase on the little table at his elbow. His voice was a raspy oratorical baritone, hard and bony like him. He was going on. "And discretion—that is essential. You have it, I know. As for me, I am a senior partner in a law firm of the highest repute, with offices at Forty Wall Street. A young woman for whom I am responsible has disappeared, and there is reason to fear that she is doing something foolish and may even be in jeopardy. She must be found as quickly as possible."

I opened a drawer to get out a notebook, and reached for my pen. What could be sweeter? A missing person, and a senior member of a Wall Street firm of high repute so bothered that he came trotting to us at night without even stopping to phone in advance. I glanced at Wolfe and suppressed a grin. His lips were tightened in resigned acceptance of the inevitable. Work was looming, work that he could probably find no rational excuse for rejecting, and how he hated it!

"I have a definite proposal," Helmar was saying. "I will pay you five thousand dollars and necessary expenses if you will find her, and put me in communication with her, by June twenty-ninth—six days from now. I will pay double that, ten thousand, if you will produce her in New York, alive and well, by the morning of June thirtieth."

My eyes were on him in fitting appreciation when he spoke of five grand, and then ten grand; but I lowered them to my notebook when I heard that date, June 30. It could have been a coincidence, but I had a good sharp hunch that it wasn't, and I have learned not to sneer at hunches. I lifted my

27

eyes enough to get Wolfe's face, but there was no sign that the date had smacked him as it had me.

He sighed good and deep, surrendering with fairly good grace to the necessity of work. "The police?" he inquired, not hopefully.

Helmar shook his head. "As I said before, discretion is essential."

"It usually is, for people who hire a private detective. Tell me about it briefly. Since you're a lawyer you should know what I need to decide whether I'll take the job."

"Why shouldn't you take it?"

"I don't know. Tell me about it."

Helmar shifted in his chair and leaned back, but not at ease. I decided that his lacing and unlacing of his fingers was not merely a habit; he was on edge. "In any case," he said, "this is confidential. The name of the young woman who has disappeared is Priscilla Eads. I have known her all her life and am her legal guardian, and also I am the trustee of her property under the will of her father, who died ten years ago. She lives in an apartment on East Seventy-fourth Street, and I was to call there this evening to discuss some business matters with her. I did so, arriving a little after eight, but she wasn't there, and the maid was alarmed, as she had expected her mistress home for an early dinner and there had been no word from her."

"I don't need that much," Wolfe said impatiently.

"Then I'll curtail it. I found on her writing desk an envelope addressed to me. Inside was a handwritten note." He reached for his briefcase and opened it. "Here it is." He took out a folded sheet of blue-tinted paper, but put it down to get a spectacle case from a pocket and put on black-rimmed glasses. He retrieved the paper. "It reads, 'Dear Perry—' "

He stopped, lifting his chin to glance at me and then at Wolfe. "She has called me by my first name," he stated, "ever since she was twelve years old and I was forty-nine. Her father suggested it."

Apparently he invited comment, and Wolfe obliged. "It is not actionable," he muttered.

Helmar nodded. "I only mention it. It reads:

"Dear Perry: I hope you won't be too mad at me for standing you up. I'm not going to do anything loony. I just want

29

to be sure where I stand. I doubt if you will hear from me before June 30, but you will then all right. Please, and I mean this, please don't try to find me.

Love, Pris."

Helmar folded the note and returned it to the briefcase. "Perhaps I should explain the significance of June thirtieth. That will be my ward's twenty-fifth birthday, and on that day, under the terms of her father's will, the trust terminates and she takes complete possession of the property. That is the basic position, but there are complications, as there always are. One is that the largest single item of the property is ninety per cent of the stock of a large and successful corporation, and there is some feeling among part of the managing and directing personnel about my ward's taking control. Another is my ward's former husband."

Wolfe frowned. "Alive?" he demanded. He refuses to touch marital messes.

"Yes." Helmar was frowning too. "That was my ward's one disastrous blunder. She ran away with him when she was nineteen, to South America, and left him three months later, and divorced him in nineteen forty-eight. There was no further communication between them, but two weeks ago I received a letter from him, sent to me as the trustee of the property, claiming that, under the provisions of a document she had signed shortly after their marriage, half of the property legally belonged to him. I doubt—"

I horned in. I had stood the suspense long enough. "You say," I blurted, "her name is Priscilla Eads?"

"Yes, she took her maiden name. The husband's name is Eric Hagh. I doubt—"

"I think I've met her. I suppose you've got a picture for us?" I got up and crossed to him. "I'd like to see."

"Certainly." He didn't care much for an underling butting in, but condescended to reach for his briefcase and finger in it. "I have three good pictures of her I brought from her apartment. Here they are." I took them and stood looking them over.

He went on. "I doubt if his claim has any legal validity, but morally—that may be a question. It is indubitably a question with my ward. His letter came from Venezuela and I think she may have gone there to see him. She fully intended—she intends—to be here on June thirtieth, but how long does it take to get from New York to Caracas by plane? Not more than twenty hours, I

31

think. She has a wild streak in her. The first thing to do will be to check all plane passengers to Venezuela, and if it's humanly possible I want to reach her before she sees that man Hagh."

I handed the photographs to Wolfe. "She's worth looking at," I told him. "Not only the pictures, but, as I thought, I've seen her. Just recently. I forget exactly where and when, but I remember from something somebody said, it was the day we had bacalhau for dinner. I don't—"

"What the devil are you gibbering about?" Wolfe demanded.

I looked him in the eye. "You heard me," I said, and sat down.

—3—

One of Wolfe's better performances was his handling of Perry Helmar after my disclosure that Priscilla Eads was upstairs in the south room. The problem was to get Helmar out of there reasonably soon with his conviction of his need for Wolfe's services intact, without any commitment from us to take his job. Wolfe broke it by telling Helmar that he would sleep on it, and that if he decided to tackle it I would call at Helmar's office at ten in the morning for further details. Of course Helmar blew up. He wanted action then and there.

"What would you think of me," Wolfe asked him, "if, solely on information furnished by you here and now, I accepted this case and started to work on it?"

"What would I think? That's what I want!"

"Surely not," Wolfe objected. "Surely you would be employing a jackass. I have never seen you before. Your name may be Perry Helmar, or it may be Eric Hagh; I have only your word for it. All that you have told me may be true, or none of it. I would like Mr. Goodwin to call on you at your office, and I would like him to visit your ward's apartment and talk with her maid. I am capable of boldness, but not of temerity. If you want the kind of detective who will dive in heedlessly on request from a stranger, Mr. Goodwin will give you some names and addresses."

Helmar was fairly stubborn and had objections and suggestions. For his identity and bona fides we could phone Richard A. Williamson. For visiting his ward's apartment and talking with her maid, tonight would do as well as tomorrow. But according to Wolfe I couldn't possibly be spared until morning because we were jointly considering an important problem, and the sooner Helmar left and let us do our considering, the better. Finally he went. He returned the photographs to the briefcase before tucking it under his arm, and in the hall he let me get his hat from the rack and open the door for him.

I went back to the office but didn't get inside. As I was stepping over the sill Wolfe barked at me, "Bring her down here!"

I stopped. "Okay. But do I brief her?"

"No. Bring her here."

I hesitated, deciding how to put it. "She's mine, you know. My taking her up and locking her in was a gag, strictly mine. You would have tossed her out if I had consulted you. You have told me to refund her dough and get rid of her. She is mine. With the dope that Helmar has kindly furnished, you will probably be much too tough for her. I reserve the right, if and when I see fit, to go up and get her luggage and take her to the door and let her out."

He chuckled audibly. He doesn't do that often, and after all the years I've been with him I haven't got the chuckle tagged. It

34

could have been anything from a gloat to an admission that I had the handle. I stood eying him for three seconds, giving him a chance to translate if he wanted it, but apparently he didn't, so I turned and strode to the stairs, mounted the two flights, inserted the key in the hole, turned it, and knocked, calling my name. Her voice told me to come in, and I opened the door and entered.

She was right at home. One of the beds had been turned down, and its coverlet, neatly folded, was on the other bed. Seated at a table near a window, under a reading lamp, doing something to her nails, she was in the blue negligee and barefooted. She looked smaller than she had in the peach-colored dress, and younger.

"I had given you up," she said, not complaining. "In another ten minutes I'll be in bed."

"I doubt it. You'll have to get dressed. Mr. Wolfe wants you down in the office."

"Now?"

"Now."

"Why can't he come up here?"

I looked at her. In that getup, to me she was a treat; to Wolfe, in his own house, she would have been an impudence. "Because there's no chair on this floor big enough for him. I'll wait outside."

I went to the hall, pulling the door to. I was not prancing or preening. True, it was I who had hooked onto something that had turned out to be worth ten grand to us, but I saw no acceptable way of cashing it in, and I had no idea what line Wolfe was going to take. I had stated my position, and he had chuckled.

It didn't take her long to dress, which scored another point for her. When she emerged, back in the peach color, she came to me, asking, "Is he very mad?"

I told her nothing alarming. The stairs are wide enough for two abreast, and we descended side by side, her fingers on my arm. That struck me as right and appropriate. I had told Wolfe that she was mine, thereby assuming a duty as well as claiming a privilege. I may have stuck out my chest some as we entered the office together, though it was involuntary.

She marched across to his desk, extended a hand, and told him cordially, "You look exactly right! Just as I thought! I would—"

She broke it off because she was getting a deep freeze. He had moved no muscle, and the expression on his face, while not belligerent, was certainly not cordial. She drew back.

He spoke. "I don't shake hands with you because you might later think it an imposition. We'll see. Sit down, Miss Eads."

She did all right, I thought. It's not a comfortable spot, having an offered hand refused, whatever the explanation may be. After drawing back, she flushed, opened her mouth and closed it, glanced at me and back at Wolfe, and, apparently deciding that restraint was called for, moved toward the red leather chair. But short of it she suddenly jerked around and demanded, "What did you call me?"

"Your name. Eads."

Flabbergasted, she stared. She transferred the stare to me. "How?" she asked, "Why didn't you tell me? But how?"

"Look," I appealed to her, "you had a jolt coming, and what did it matter whether from him or me? Sit down and take it."

"But you couldn't possibly . . ." It trailed off. She moved and sat. Her remarkable eyes went to Wolfe. "Not that it makes much difference. I suppose I'll have to pay you more, but I was willing to anyhow. I told Mr. Goodwin so."

Wolfe nodded. "And he told you that he

was taking the money you gave him tentatively, conditional on my approval. Archie, get it, please, and return it to her."

I had expected that, naturally, and had decided not to make an issue of it. If and when I took a stand I wanted to be on the best ground in sight. So I arose and crossed to the safe and opened it, got the seven new fifties, went to Priscilla, and proffered them. She didn't lift a hand.

"Take it," I advised her. "If you want to balk, pick a better spot." I dropped it on her lap and returned to my chair. As I sat down, Wolfe was speaking.

"Your presence here, Miss Eads, is preposterous. This is neither a rooming house nor an asylum for hysterical women; it is my—"

"I'm not hysterical!"

"Very well, I withdraw it. It is not an asylum for unhysterical women; it is my office and my home. For you to come here and ask to be allowed to stay a week, sleeping and eating in the room directly above mine, without revealing your identity or any of the circumstances impelling you, was grotesque. Mr. Goodwin knew that, and you would have been promptly ejected if he had not chosen to use you and your fantastic request as a means of badgering me—and also, of course, if you had not been young and attractive. Because he did so choose, and you are uncommonly attractive, you were actually taken up to a room and helped to unpack, refreshments were taken up to you, a meal was served you, my whole household was disrupted. Then—"

"I'm sorry." Priscilla's face was good and red, no faint pink flush. "I'm extremely sorry. I'll leave at once." She was rising.

Wolfe showed her a palm. "If you please. There has been a development. We have had a visitor. He left here only half an hour ago. A man named Perry Helmar."

She gasped. "Perry!" She dropped back into the chair. "You told him I'm here!"

"No." Wolfe was curt. "He had been to your apartment and found you gone, and had found the note you left for him—you did leave a note for him?"

"I—yes."

"Finding it, and learning you had scooted, he came straight here. He wanted to hire me to find you. He told me of your approaching twenty-fifth birthday, and of the communication he received recently from your former husband, now in Venezuela, regarding a document you once signed, giving him half of your property. You did sign such a document?"

"Yes."

"Wasn't that a foolish thing to do?"

"Yes, but I was a fool then, so naturally I was foolish."

"Well. When Mr. Goodwin looked at photographs of you Mr. Helmar had brought, of course he recognized you, and he managed to inform me without informing Mr. Helmar. But Mr. Helmar had already made a definite proposal. He offered to pay me ten thousand dollars and expenses if I would produce you in New York, alive and well, by the morning of June thirtieth."

"Produce me?" Priscilla laughed, but not merrily.

"That was his phrase." Wolfe leaned back and rubbed his lip with a fingertip. "The moment Mr. Goodwin recognized the photographs and informed me, I was of course in an anomalous situation. I earn a living and maintain an expensive establishment by working as a private detective. I can't afford quixotism. When I am offered a proper fee for a legitimate job in the field I cover, I don't refuse it. I need the money. So. A man I've never seen before comes and offers me ten thousand dollars to find and produce a certain object by a certain date, and by chance—by chance alone—that object is locked in a room of my house. Is there any reason why I shouldn't disclose it to him and collect my fee?"

"I see." She pressed her lips together. In a moment the tip of her tongue showed, going from left to right and back again. "That's how it is. It was lucky he brought the photographs for Mr. Goodwin to recognize, wasn't it?" Her eyes moved to me. "I suppose I should congratulate you, Mr. Goodwin?"

"It's too early to tell," I growled. "Save it."

"I admit," Wolfe told her, "that if I had accepted a commission from you, or if Mr. Goodwin, acting as my agent, had taken money from you unconditionally, I would be bound to your interest and therefore unable to consider Mr. Helmar's offer. But there is no such bond. I am not committed to you in any way. There was no legal, professional, or ethical obstacle to prevent my disclosing you to him and demanding payment—but, confound it, there was my self-esteem. And is. I can't do it. Also there is Mr. Goodwin. I have rebuked him for installing you and told him to get rid of

41

you, and if I now collect ransom for you he will be impossible to live with or work with."

Wolfe shook his head. "So it is by no means my good fortune that you chose my house as a haven. If you had gone anywhere else, Mr. Helmar would have come to hire me to find you, I would have taken the job, and I would surely have earned the fee. If my self-esteem will not let me profit by your presence here, through chance and Mr. Goodwin, neither will my self-interest permit me to suffer loss by it—so substantial a loss—and I have two suggestions to offer— alternative suggestions. The first is simple. When you were arranging with Mr. Goodwin to stay here you told him in effect that there was no limit to the amount you would pay. Your words, as he reported them to me, were, 'Whatever you say.' You were speaking to him as my agent, and therefore to me. I now say ten thousand dollars."

She goggled at him, her brows high. "You mean *I* pay you ten thousand dollars?"

"Yes. I submit this comment: I suspect that the money will come from you in any case, directly or indirectly. If, as the trustee of your property, Mr. Helmar has wide discretion, as he probably has, it is more than likely that the payment for finding and pro-

42

ducing you would come from that property, so actually—"

"This is blackmail!"

"I doubt if you can properly—"

"It's blackmail! You're saying that if I don't pay you ten thousand dollars you'll tell Perry Helmar I'm here and get it from him!"

"I'm saying no such thing." Wolfe was being patient. "I said I had an alternative suggestion. If you don't like that one here's the other." He looked at the wall clock. "It's ten minutes past eleven. Mr. Goodwin helped you unpack; he can help you pack. You can be out of here in five minutes, with your luggage, and there will be no surveillance. We will not even so much as spy from a window to see which way you turn. We will forget you exist for ten hours and forty-five minutes. At the end of that period, at ten o'clock tomorrow morning, I shall phone Mr. Helmar, take his job on the terms he proposed, and start after you."

Wolfe fluttered a hand. "It was distasteful to me, having to offer to take the money direct from you instead of through Mr. Helmar, but I felt you merited that consideration. I'm glad you contemn it as blackmail, since I like to pretend that I earn at least a fraction of what I collect; but the offer stands until ten in the morning, should you decide that you prefer it to this hide-and-seek."

"I'm not going to pay you any ten thousand dollars!" She had her chin up.

"Good."

"It's ridiculous!"

"I agree. Also, of course, the alternative is ridiculous for me. Leaving here, you can go straight home, phone Mr. Helmar that you are there and will see him in the morning, and go to bed, leaving me to go whistle for my dinner. I'll have to risk that; there's no way around it."

"I'm not going home, and I'm not going to phone anyone."

"As you please." Wolfe glanced at the clock. "It's a quarter past eleven, and you have no time to lose if you expect to make it a job for me. Archie, will you bring her luggage down, please?"

I arose, in no hurry. The situation was highly unsatisfactory, but how could I change it? Priscilla wasn't waiting. She was out of her chair, saying, "I can manage, thanks," and on her way.

I watched her crossing the hall and starting up, and then turned to Wolfe. "It reminds me more of 'run sheep run,' as we called it in Ohio. That's what the shepherd yelled—'run sheep run!' It ought to be an exciting game and lots of fun, but I think I should tell you before she leaves, I'm not absolutely sure I'll want to play. You may have to fire me."

He only muttered, "Get her out of here."

I took my time mounting the stairs, thinking she wouldn't want my help folding things. The door to the south room was standing open. From the landing I called, "May I come in?"

"Don't bother," her voice came. "I'll make out."

She was moving around. I went to the threshold. The suitcase, open on the rack, was three-fourths packed. That girl would have been a very satisfactory traveling companion. Without a glance at me, she finished the suitcase, swift and efficient, and started on the hatbox.

"Watch your money," I said. "You have plenty. Don't give it to a stranger to hold."

"Sending little sister off to camp?" she asked, without giving me the eyes. It may have been banter, but it wasn't any too light.

"Yeah. Down there you said you supposed you should congratulate me, and I asked you to save it. I doubt if I deserve it."

"I guess you don't. I take it back."

She pulled the zipper all the way around the hatbox, got her jacket and hat and put them on, and took her handbag from the table. She reached for the hatbox, but I already had it, and also the suitcase. She went first, and I followed. Down in the lower hall she didn't glance into the office as we passed by, but I did, and saw Wolfe at his desk, leaning back with his eyes closed. When I had the front door open she made to take the luggage, but I hung on to it. She persisted but so did I, and since I weighed more I won. At the foot of the stoop we turned east, walked to Tenth Avenue, and crossed to the other side.

"I will not," I told her, "file the brand and number of the taxi, or if I do I won't report it or refer to it. However, I am making no promise that I will permanently forget your name. Some day I may think of something I'll want to ask you. If I don't see you before June thirtieth, happy birthday."

We parted on those terms—not exactly gushy, but not implacable. After watching her taxi roll off uptown, I walked back to the house, expecting an extended session with Wolfe, and not with any uncontrollable glee. It was an interesting situation, I was willing to hand him that, but I wasn't at all sure I liked my part. However, I found that I was to be allowed to sleep on it. By the time I got back Wolfe had gone up to bed, which suited me fine.

The next morning, Tuesday, there was a clash. I was having orange juice and griddle cakes and grilled Georgia ham and honey and coffee and melon and more coffee in the kitchen, as usual, when Fritz came back down from taking Wolfe's breakfast tray up to him and said I was wanted. That was according to precedent. Since Wolfe didn't come downstairs before going up to the plant rooms at nine o'clock, his habit was to send for me if he had morning instructions not suited to the house phone. Fritz said nothing had been said about urgency, so I finished my second cup of coffee without gulping and then went up the one flight to Wolfe's room, directly under the one Priscilla had not slept in. He had finished breakfast and was out of bed, standing by a window in his two acres of yellow pajamas, massaging his scalp with his fingertips. I wished him good morning, and he was good enough to reciprocate.

"What time is it?" he demanded.

There were two clocks in the room, one on his bed table and one on the wall not ten feet from where he was standing, but I humored him, looking at my wrist.

"Eight thirty-two."

"Please get Mr. Helmar at his office sharp at ten o'clock and put him through to me upstairs. It would be pointless for you to go there, since we are more up-to-date than he is. Meanwhile it won't hurt to ring Miss Eads' apartment to learn if she's at home. Unless you already have?"

"No, sir."

"Then try it. If she's not there we should be prepared to waste no time. Get after Saul, Fred, and Orrie at once, and tell them to be here by eleven o'clock if possible."

I shook my head, regretfully but firmly. "No, sir. I warned you that you may have to fire me. I don't refuse to play, but I will not help with any fudging. You told her that we would forget her existence until ten this morning. I have done so. I have no idea who or what you're talking about. Do you want me to come upstairs at ten o'clock to see if you have any instructions?"

"No," he snapped, and headed for the bathroom. Reaching it and opening the door, he yelled at me over his shoulder, "I mean yes!" and disappeared within. To save Fritz a trip, I took the breakfast tray down with me.

Ordinarily, unless there is a job on, I don't go to the office until the morning mail comes, somewhere between 8:45 and nine o'clock. So when the doorbell rang a little before nine I was still in the kitchen, discussing the Giants and Dodgers with Fritz. Going through to the hall and proceeding toward the front, I stopped dead when I saw through the one-way glass who it was.

I'm just reporting. As far as I know, no electrons had darted in either direction when I first laid eyes on Priscilla Eads, nor had I felt faint or dizzy at any point during my association with her, but the fact remains that I have never had swifter or stronger hunches than the two that were connected with her. Monday evening, before Helmar had said much more than twenty words about his missing ward, I had said to myself, "She's upstairs," and knew it. Tuesday morning, when I saw Inspector Cramer of Manhattan Homicide on the stoop, I said to myself, "She's dead," and knew it. Halting,

I stood three seconds before advancing to open the door.

I greeted him. He said, "Hello, Goodwin," strode in and past me, and on to the office. I followed and crossed to my desk, noting that instead of going for the red leather chair he was taking a yellow one, indicating that I and not Wolfe was it this time. I told him that Wolfe would not be available for two hours, which he knew already, since he was as familiar with the schedule as I was.

"Will I do?" I asked.

"You will for a start," he growled. "Last night a woman was murdered, and your fresh fingerprints are on her luggage. How did they get there?"

I met his eye. "That's no way to do it," I objected. "My fingerprints could be found on women's luggage from Maine to California. Name and address and description of luggage?"

"Priscilla Eads, Six-eighteen East Seventy-fourth Street. A suitcase and a hatbox, both light tan leather."

"She was murdered?"

"Yes. Your prints were fresh. How come?"

Inspector Cramer was no Sir Laurence

Olivier, but I would not previously have called him ugly. At that moment it suddenly struck me that he was ugly. His big round face always got redder in the summertime, and seemed to be puffier, making his eyes appear smaller but no less quick and sharp. "Like a baboon," I said.

"What?"

"Nothing." I swiveled and buzzed the plant rooms on the house phone, and in a moment Wolfe answered.

"Inspector Cramer is here," I told him. "A woman named Priscilla Eads has been murdered, and Cramer says my fingerprints are on her luggage and wants to know how come. Have I ever heard of her?"

"Confound it."

"Yes, sir. I double. Do you want to come down here?"

"No."

"Shall we go up there?"

"No. You know all that I do."

"I sure do. So I unload?"

"Certainly. Why not?"

"Yeah, why not. She's dead."

I hung up and turned to Cramer.

—4—

I am inclined to believe that Cramer has a fairly good understanding of Wolfe in most respects, but not all. For instance, he exaggerates Wolfe's appetite for dough, which I suppose is natural, since if he goes on being an honest cop, which he is, the most he can ever expect to get is considerably less than Wolfe pays me, whereas Wolfe's annual take is well up in six figures. I admit Wolfe is not in business for my health, but he is quite capable of letting a customer leave the premises with a dime for carfare or even a buck for a taxi.

However, Cramer is not under that impression, and therefore, when he learned that we had no client connected in any way with Priscilla Eads, now that she was dead, and apparently no prospect of any, and hence no fee to build up and safeguard, he started calling me Archie, which had happened before, but not often. He expressed appreciation for the information I provided, taking a dozen pages of notes in his small neat hand, and asking plenty of questions, not to challenge but just to elucidate. He did offer a pointed comment about what he called our dodge with Helmar, with his ward upstairs, and I rebutted.

"Okay," I told him, "you name it. She came here uninvited, and so did he. We had made no engagement with either one. They couldn't both have what they wanted. Let's hear how you would have handled it."

"I'm not a genius like Wolfe. He could have been too busy to consider taking Helmar's job."

"And use what to meet his payroll? Speaking of busy, are you too busy to answer a question from a citizen in good standing?"

He looked at his wrist. "I'm due at the DA's office at ten-thirty."

"Then we've got hours—anyhow, minutes. Why did you want to make it so tight about the time Helmar left here? It was shortly after ten, and it was more than an hour later that Miss Eads left."

"Uh-huh." He got out a cigar. "What paper do you read?"

"The *Times*, but today I've seen only page one and sports."

"It didn't make the *Times*. A little after one o'clock last night the body of a woman was found in a vestibule on East Twenty-ninth Street. She had been strangled with some kind of cord, not very thick. There was trouble identifying her because her bag had been taken, but she lived in a nearby tenement and it didn't take too long. Her name was Margaret Fomos, and she worked as a maid at the apartment of Miss Priscilla Eads on Seventy-fourth Street. It was a full-time job, but she lived on Twenty-ninth Street with her husband. She usually got home around nine, but last evening she phoned her husband that she wouldn't arrive until eleven. He says she sounded upset, and he asked her why, and she said she would tell him when she saw him."

"So she was killed about eleven o'clock?"

"Not known. The building on Seventy-fourth Street is a private house done over into luxes, one to a floor, except Miss Eads—she had the two top floors—and the elevator is self-service, so there is no staff around to see people coming and going. The ME puts it between ten-thirty and midnight."

Cramer glanced at his wrist, stuck the cigar between his teeth at the left corner of his mouth, and clamped down on it. He never lit one. "I was home in bed. Rowcliff took it. He had four men on it, following routine, and around four o'clock one of them, a young fellow named Auerbach, decided he had brains and he might as well give 'em a chance. It occurred to him that he had never heard of a bag-snatcher going so far as to strangle the victim, and there was no evidence of any attempt at rape. What was there about her, or about the bag, that called for strangling? According to the husband, nothing about her, nor the bag either. But listing the contents of the bag as well as he could with the husband's help, one item struck Auerbach as worth considering—Mrs. Fomos's key to the apartment where she worked.

"He'll have your job someday."

"He's welcome to it now. He went to Seventy-fourth Street and rang the bell to the Eads apartment and got no answer. He got the janitor and had him open the door and take a look. The body of Priscilla Eads was there on the floor, half in a bathroom and half in a hall. She had been hit on the side of the head with the poker from her fireplace and then strangled with some kind of cord, not very thick. Her hat was lying near her, and she had her jacket on, so he had probably been there waiting for her when she came in. We'll know more about

55

that when we find the hackie, which should be soon with what you gave me. The ME puts it between one and two."

"Then she didn't go straight home. As I told you, I put her in the taxi about twenty to twelve."

"I know. Auerbach got Rowcliff, and the boys moved in. The crop of prints was below average—I guess Mrs. Fomos was a good cleaner and duster—and the best of the lot were some nice fresh ones on the luggage. When the word came that they were yours Rowcliff phoned me, and I decided to drop by here on my way downtown. He doesn't know how to handle Wolfe at all, and you have the same effect on him as a bee on a dog's nose."

"Some day I'll describe the effect he has on me."

"I'd rather not." Cramer looked at his wrist. "I had it in mind to have a word with Wolfe, but I know how he is about being disturbed up there about a little thing like a homicide, and I'd just as soon take it from you, so long as I get it."

"You've got it all right."

"I believe you, for a change." He left his chair. "Especially since he has no client, and none in sight that I can see. He'll be in one hell of a humor, and I don't envy you. I'll be going. You understand you're a material and you'll be around."

I said I would.

When I went back down the hall after letting Cramer out I started to re-enter the office, but suddenly braked at the door, pivoted, and made for the stairs. Two flights up, I went into the south room, stood in its center, and looked around. Fritz hadn't been in it yet, and the bed was turned down as Priscilla had left it, with the folded coverlet on the other bed. I went and lifted the coverlet to look under it and dropped it again. I raised the pillow on the turned-down bed and glanced under that. I crossed to the large bureau between the windows and started opening and closing drawers.

I was not being completely cuckoo. I was a trained and experienced detective, there had been a murder that I was interested in and wanted to know more about, and the closest I could get to it at the moment was this room in which Priscilla had expected to sleep and eat her breakfast. I hadn't the slightest expectation of finding anything helpful, and so wasn't disappointed when I didn't; and I did find something at that. On a shelf in the bathroom was a toothbrush

57

and a soiled handkerchief. I took them to my room and put them on my dresser, and I still have them, in a drawer where I keep a collection of assorted professional relics.

There was no point in going up to the plant rooms and starting a squabble, so I went down to the office and opened the morning mail and fiddled around with chores. Somewhat later, when I became aware that I was entering a germination date of Cymbidium holfordianum on the card of Cymbidium pauwelsi, I decided I wasn't in the mood for clerical work, returned things to the files, and sat and stared at my toes. There were four thousand things I wanted to know, and there were people I might have started asking, like Sergeant Purley Stebbins or Lon Cohen of the *Gazette*, but after all this was Nero Wolfe's office and phone.

At eleven o'clock he came down, entered and crossed to his desk, got himself settled in his chair, and glanced through the little stack of mail I had put there under a paper-weight. There was nothing of much interest and certainly nothing urgent. He cocked his head, focused on me, and stated, "It would have been like you to come up at ten o'clock for instructions as arranged."

I nodded. "I know, but Cramer didn't leave until five after, and I knew how you would react. Do you care to hear the details?"

"Go ahead."

I gave him what I had got from Cramer. When I had finished he sat frowning at me with his eyes half closed, through a long silence. Finally he spoke. "You reported in full to Mr. Cramer?"

"I did. You said to unload."

"Yes. Then Mr. Helmar will soon know, if he doesn't already, of our stratagem, and I doubt if it's worth the trouble to communicate with him. He wanted his ward alive and well, so he said, and that's out of the question."

I disagreed, not offensively. "But he's our only contact, and, no matter how sore he is, we can start with him. We have to start somewhere with someone."

"Start?" He was peevish. "Start what? For whom? We have no client. There's nothing to start."

The simple and direct thing to do would have been to blow my top, and it would have been a satisfaction—but then what? I refused to boil, and kept my voice even. "I don't deny," I told him, "that that's one

59

way to look at it, but only one, and there is at least one other. Like this. She was here and wanted to stay, and we kicked her out, and she got killed. I should think that would have some bearing on your self-esteem, which you were discussing last night. I should think that you do have something to start—a murder investigation. And you also have a client—your self-esteem."

"Nonsense!"

"Maybe." I stayed calm. "I would like to explain at length why I think it's up to us to get the guy that killed Priscilla Eads, but I don't want to waste your time or my breath just for the hell of it. Would it do any good?"

"No."

"You won't even consider it?"

"Why should I?" He fluttered a hand. "I am under no onus and am offered no reward. No."

"Okay," I stood up. "I guess I knew how it would be. You realize that I have my personal problem, and it's different from yours. If I had turned her down and put her out yesterday afternoon as soon as I found out what she wanted, would she be in the morgue now? I doubt it. When you came down and I sprung her on you, you told me

60

to get her out of the house before dinner. If I had, would she be in the morgue now? Probably not. It was absolutely my fault that she didn't leave until nearly midnight, and she decided to go home, it doesn't matter why. It may have been just to change her clothes and luggage, or she may have decided not to play—anyhow, she went home, and she got it. That's my personal problem."

"Archie." He was gruff. "No man can hold himself accountable for the results of his psychological defects, especially those he shares with all his fellow men, such as lack of omniscience. It is a vulgar fallacy that what you don't know can't hurt you; but it is true that what you don't know can't convict you."

"It's still my personal problem. I can get along without omniscience, but I can't get along with a goddam strangler going around being grateful to me for sending his victim to him, and I don't intend to try. I'll quit if you prefer it, but I'd rather take an indefinite leave of absence, starting now—without pay, of course. You can get Saul in. I'll move to a hotel, but I suppose you won't mind if I drop in occasionally in case I need something."

61

He was glowering at me. "Do I under-stand you? Do you intend to go single-handed for the murderer of Miss Eads?"

"I don't know about single-handed. I may need some hired help, but I'm going for him."

"Pfui." He was contemptuous. "Pop-pycock. Is Mr. Cramer such a bungler? And his men? So inept that you must assume their functions?"

I stared at him. "I'll be damned. That, from you?"

He shook his head. "It won't do, Archie. You're trying to coerce me, and I won't have it. I will not undertake a major and expensive operation, with no chance of in-come, merely because you have been piqued by circumstance. Your bluff won't work. It would of course be folly for you to try any—what's that for?"

I was too busy to answer him. With my jacket off, I had got a shoulder holster from a drawer and was strapping it on. That done, I took a Marley .32 and a box of cartridges, filled the cylinder, put the gun in the holster, and put my jacket back on. It was an effective retort to Wolfe, but that was not the sole reason for it. Ever since a certain regrettable experience some years back, I never left the house on an errand connected with a murder case without taking a gun, so I was merely following habit.

I faced Wolfe. "I'll do my best to see that everybody understands that I'm not working for you. Some of them won't believe it, but I can't help that. I'll come back for some things, and if I can't make it until late I'll phone to tell you what hotel I'm at. If you decide you'd rather have me quit, okay. I haven't got time to discuss it now because I want to catch a guy before lunch."

He sat with his lips pressed tight, scowling. I turned and went. Passing the hall rack, I snared my straw hat, not that I don't hate to monkey with a hat in summer, but I might need the tone. Descending the seven steps of the stoop, I turned east as if I knew exactly where I was headed for, walked to Tenth Avenue and turned downtown, and at the corner of Thirty-fourth Street entered a drugstore, mounted a stool at the soda fountain, and ordered a chocolate egg malted with three eggs.

There was no guy I wanted to catch before lunch. I had got away from there because I knew I had to as soon as I saw there was no chance of harassing Wolfe into taking a hand. I didn't blame him; he had no personal problem like mine. I wasn't fussing about the problem. That was settled. Until further notice I had only one use for my time and faculties: to find out who the strangler was that I had sent Priscilla Eads to in a taxi, and wrap him up for delivery to the proper address, with or without help. I had no great ideas about galloping down Broadway on a white horse with his head on the point of a spear. I just wanted to catch the sonofabitch, or at least help.

I considered the notion of helping. I could go to Inspector Cramer, explain my problem, and offer to stick strictly to orders if he would take me on as a special for the case. I might have done it but for the fact that Rowcliff would probably be giving some of the orders. Nothing on earth could justify a man's deliberately putting himself under orders from Rowcliff. I gave that up. But then what? If I went to Priscilla's apartment I wouldn't be let in. If I got to Perry Helmar, supposing I could, he wouldn't speak to me. I had to find a crack somewhere.

When I had finished the malted, and a glass of water for a chaser, I went to a phone booth, dialed the number of the *Gazette*, and got Lon Cohen.

"First," I told him, "this call is strictly

personal. Nero Wolfe is neither involved nor interested. With that understood, kindly tell me all facts, surmises, and rumors connected directly or indirectly with Miss Priscilla Eads and her murder."

"The paper costs a nickel, son. I'm busy."

"So am I. I can't wait for the paper. Did she leave any relatives?"

"None in New York that we know of. A couple of aunts in California."

"Have you got any kind of a line that you can mention on the phone?"

"Yes and no. Nothing exclusive. You know about her father's will?"

"I know absolutely nothing."

"Her mother died when she was an infant, and her father when she was fifteen. The cash and securities he left her, and the insurance, were nothing spectacular, but he set up a trust of ninety per cent of the stock of Softdown, Incorporated, a ten-million-dollar towel and textile business. The trustee was his friend and lawyer, Perry Helmar. Eighty per cent of the income of the trust was to go to Priscilla, and on her twenty-fifth birthday the whole works was to become her property. In case she died before her twenty-fifth birthday, the stock was to become the property of the officers and em-

65

ployees of the corporation. They were named in a schedule that was part of the will, with the amount to go to each one. Most of it went in big gobs to less than a dozen of them. Okay, she was killed six days before her twenty-fifth birthday. That is obviously a line, but it's certainly not exclusive."

"I'll bet it's not. The damn fool—I mean the father. What about the guy she married? I hear she ran away with him. Who was she running from? Her father was dead."

"I don't know—maybe the trustee; he was her guardian. That wasn't here. She met him somewhere on a trip, down South I think. There's very little on it in New York. What do you mean, Wolfe is neither involved nor interested?"

"Just that. He isn't."

"Ha-ha. I suppose you're calling for a friend. Give him my regards. Have you got your dime's worth?"

"For now, yes. I'll buy you a steak at Pierre's at seven-thirty."

He made a smacking noise. "That's the best offer I've had today. I hope I can make it. Ring me at seven?"

"Right. Much obliged."

I hung up, pulled the door open, and got out a handkerchief and wiped my brow and behind, my ears. The booth was hot. I stepped out, found the Manhattan phone book, looked up an address, went out and crossed Thirty-fourth Street, and got a taxi going east.

—5—

The headquarters of Softdown, Incorporated, at 192 Collins Street, in the middle of the ancient jungle between City Hall Park and Greenwich Village, was not an office or a floor, it was a building. Its four-storied front may once have been cream-colored brick, but you would have had to use a chisel or a sand-blaster to find out. However, the two enormous street-floor windows, one on either side of the entrance, were so bright and clean they sparkled. Behind one was a vast geometrical array of bathtowels, in a dozen colors and twice that many sizes, and behind the other was a crazy old contraption with a placard resting on one of its crosspieces which said:

HARGREAVES' SPINNING JENNY
1768

Both sides of the double door were standing open, and I entered. The left half of the wide and deep room was partitioned off all the way back, with a string of doors, but the right half was open, with an army of tables, piled with merchandise. Only four or five people were in sight, scattered around. An opening in the first eight feet of partition had the word INFORMATION above it, but the old war mare inside, seated at a switchboard, looked too damn skeptical, and I went on by, to the right, to where a rotund and ruddy type stood scratching the top of his ear. I showed him my case, open to display my license card with its photograph, and snapped, "Goodwin. Detective. Where's the boss?"

He barely glanced at it. "Which boss?" he squeaked. "What do you want?"

Another skeptic. "Relax," I told him in an official tone. "I'm on an errand connected with the death of Priscilla Eads. I want to talk with everyone here who will own part of this business because she died, preferably starting at the top. Would it be better to start with you? Your name, please."

He didn't bat an eye. "You want to see Mr. Brucker," he squeaked.

"I agree. Where is he?"

"His office is down at the end, but right now he's upstairs in the conference room."

"And the stairs?"

He jerked a thumb. "Over there."

I went in the direction indicated and through a door. Everything about the stairs was contemporary with the building except the treads and risers, which were up-to-date rough-top plastic. The second floor was visibly a busier place than the first. There were row after row of desks with typewriters and other machines, cabinets and shelves, and of course the girls, easily a hundred of them. There is no more agreeable form of research than the study of animated contour, color, and motion in a large business office, but that day I was preoccupied. I crossed to a dark-eyed smooth-skinned creature manipulating a machine bigger than her, and asked where the conference room was, and she pointed to the far end of the room, away from the street. I went there, found a door in a partition, opened it and passed through, and closed the door behind me.

The partition was well soundproofed, for as soon as I shut the door the clatter and hum of the big room's activity became just a murmur. This room was of medium size, square, with a fine old mahogany table in the middle, and chairs to match all the way around it. At the far side was a stairhead. One of the five people seated in a cluster at the end of the table could have been Hargreaves of the 1768 spinning jenny, or anyhow his son, with his pure white hair and his wrinkled old skin trying to find room enough for itself with the face meat gone. He still had sharp blue-gray eyes, and they drew me in his direction as I displayed my case and said, "Goodwin. Detective. About the murder of Priscilla Eads. Mr. Brucker?"

Whitey was not Brucker. Brucker was the one across from him, about half Whitey's age and with half as much hair, light brown, and a long pale face and a long thin nose. He spoke. "I'm Brucker. What do you want?"

None of them was reaching for the case, so I returned it to my pocket, got onto a chair, and took out my notebook and pencil. I was thinking that if I didn't overplay my self-assurance I might get away with it. I opened the notebook and flipped to a fresh page, in no hurry, and ran my eyes over them, ending at Brucker. "This is only a preliminary," I told him. "Full name, please."

"J. Luther Brucker."

"What does the J. stand for?"

"It's J-a-y, Jay."

I was writing. "You're an officer of the corporation?"

"President. I have been for seven years."

"When and how did you learn of the murder of Miss Eads?"

"On the radio this morning. The seven-forty-five newscast."

"That was the first you heard of it?"

"Yes."

"How did you spend your time last night between ten-thirty and two o'clock? Briefly. As fast as you please. I do shorthand."

"I was in bed. I was tired after a hard day's work and went to bed early, shortly after ten, and stayed there."

"Where do you live?"

"I have a suite at the Prince Henry Hotel, Brooklyn."

I looked at him. I always look again at people who live in Brooklyn. "Is that where you were last night?"

"Certainly. That's where my bed is, and I was in it."

"Alone?"

"I'm unmarried."

"Were you alone in your suite throughout the period from ten-thirty to two o'clock last night?"

"I was."

"Can you furnish any corroboration? Phone calls? Anything at all?"

His jaw moved spasmodically. He was controlling himself. "How can I? I was asleep."

I looked at him without bias but with reserve. "You understand the situation, Mr. Brucker. A lot of people stand to profit from Miss Eads' death, some of them substantially. These things have to be asked about. How much of this business will you now inherit?"

"That's a matter of public record."

"Yeah. But you know, don't you?"

"Of course I know."

"Then, if you don't mind, how much?"

"Under the provisions of the will of the late Nathan Eads, son of the founder of the business, I suppose that nineteen thousand three hundred and sixty-two shares of the common stock of the corporation will come to me. The same amount will go to four other people—Miss Duday, Mr. Quest, Mr.

72

Pitkin, and Mr. Helmar. Smaller amounts go to others."

Whitey spoke, his sharp blue-gray eyes straight at me. "I am Bernard Quest." His voice was firm and strong, with no sign of wrinkles. "I have been with this business sixty-two years, and have been sales manager for thirty-four years and vice-president for twenty-nine."

"Right." I wrote. "I'll get names down." I looked at the woman next to Bernard Quest on his left. She was middle-aged, with a scrawny neck and dominating ears, and was unquestionably a rugged individualist, since no lipstick had been allowed anywhere near her. I asked her, "Yours, please?"

"Viola Duday," she said in a clear voice so surprisingly pleasant that I raised my brows at my notebook. "I was Mr. Eads' secretary, and in nineteen thirty-nine he made me assistant to the president. He was, of course, president. During his last illness, the last fourteen months of his life, I ran the business."

"We helped all we could," Brucker said pointedly.

She ignored him. "My present title," she told me, "is assistant secretary of the corporation."

I moved my eyes. "You, sir?"

That one, on Viola Duday's left, was a neat little squirt, with a suspicious twist to his lips, who had been fifty years old all his life and would be for the rest of it. Apparently he had a cold, since he kept sniffing and dabbing at his nose with a handkerchief.

"Oliver Pitkin," he said, and was a little hoarse. "Secretary and treasurer of the corporation since nineteen thirty-seven, when my predecessor died at the age of eighty-two."

I was beginning to suspect that the conference I had crashed had not been about the price of towels. Of the four Brucker had named besides himself, three were present—all but Helmar. That proved nothing against any or all of them, but I wished I had a recording of their conversation before I entered. Not that I wasn't doing all right, considering. I focused on the only one still nameless, and the only one of the five who could have been regarded as worthy of attention on other grounds than her possible connection with the murder of Priscilla Eads. As for age, she could have been Bernard Quest's granddaughter. As for structure, she could have been improved upon—who

74

couldn't?—but no part of her called for a motion to reconsider. A tendency of Brucker's head to twist toward his right, where she sat, had not been unnoticed by me. I asked her for her name.

"Daphne O'Neil," she said. "But I don't think I belong in your little book, Mr. Detective, because I wasn't in Mr. Eads' will. I was just a good little girl when he died, and I only started to work for Softdown four years ago. Now I'm the Softdown stylist."

The way she produced words it wasn't exactly baby talk, but it gave you the feeling that in four seconds it would be. Also she called me Mr. Detective, which settled it that a Softdown stylist should be seen and not heard.

"Perhaps you should know," Viola Duday volunteered in her clear, pleasant voice, "that if Miss Eads had lived until next Monday and controlled the business, Miss O'Neil would soon have been looking for another connection. Miss Eads did not appreciate Miss O'Neil's talents. You may think it generous of Miss O'Neil not to want you to waste space on her in your little book, but—"

"Is this necessary, Vi?" Bernard Quest asked sharply.

"I think so." She was pleasantly firm about it. "Being an intelligent woman, Bernie, I'm more realistic than any man, even you. No one is going to be able to hide anything, so why not shorten the agony? They'll dig up everything. That for ten years before Nate Eads died you tried to get him to give you a third interest in the business, and he refused. That Ollie here"—she glanced, not with animosity, at Oliver Pitkin—"beneath his mask of modest and stubborn efficiency, is fiercely anti-feminist and hates to see a woman own or run anything."

"My dear Viola," Pitkin began in a shocked tone, but she overspoke him.

"That my ambition and appetite for power are so strong that you four men, much as you fear and distrust one another, fear and distrust me more, and you knew that when Priscilla was in control I would have top authority. They'll learn that this Daphne O'Neil—my God, what a name for her, Daphne—"

"It means 'laurel tree,' " Daphne said to be helpful.

"I know it does. That she was playing Perry Helmar and Jay against each other, and with June thirtieth approaching she was getting desperate and so were they. That Jay—"

What stopped her was Daphne suddenly reaching across in front of Pitkin and slapping her on the mouth. It was a remarkably swift and accurate performance, giving Viola Duday no time to duck or block. Miss Duday raised a hand as if to counter, but merely covered her mouth with it, recoiling.

"You asked for it, Vi," Quest told her. "And if you're counting on Ollie and me being with you, and I think you are, this is a big mistake."

"I've been wanting to do it for a long time," said Daphne, more like baby talk than before. "I'll do it again."

I was perfectly willing to sit and wait for Miss Duday to start up where she had left off, or for someone else to start something, but apparently that script was finished, so I spoke.

"Miss Duday is absolutely right," I told them. "I don't mean that what she said is right—that I don't know about—but she was right in saying that if you try to hold out and cover up you'll just prolong the agony. It'll all come out, don't think it won't, the bad with the good, and the quicker the better." I looked at the president. "It wouldn't hurt a bit, Mr. Brucker, if you followed Miss Duday's example. Where does everybody stand, the way you see it? For instance, this conference you were having. Whose idea was it? What were you talking about? What were you saying?"

Brucker, his head tilted back, was regarding me down his long, thin nose. "We were saying," he stated, "that we would have to accept the fact that the manner of Miss Eads' death, especially at this time, created an extremely unpleasant situation for all of us. I had spoken to Mr. Quest about it, and we had decided to discuss it with Miss Duday and Mr. Pitkin. I had already spoken with Miss O'Neil and thought she should be present. We agreed that it was unthinkable that any of us, or any other member of the Softdown staff who will now come into possession of Softdown stock, could possibly have been involved in the murder of Miss Eads. We—"

"Miss Duday agreed to that?"

She answered me. "Certainly. If you thought, young man, that I was suggesting motives for murder acceptable to me you misunderstood. I was merely giving you facts which will seem to you to be acceptable motives for murder. You were sure to discover them, and I was saving time."

"I see. What else were you saying, Mr. Brucker?"

"We were considering what to do. Specifically, we were considering whether we should arrange at once to get legal advice, and if so whether our corporation counsel would do, or would it be better to have special counsel for this. Also we were discussing the murder itself. We agreed that we knew of no one with a reason for killing Miss Eads and capable of such a crime. We spoke of the letter received recently from Eric Hagh, Miss Eads' former husband, by Perry Helmar—you know about that?"

"Yes, from Helmar. Claiming that he had a document that entitled him to half of her property."

"That's right. The letter was sent from Venezuela, but he could have come to New York by ship or plane—or he didn't even have to come; he could have hired someone to kill her."

"I see. Why?"

"We don't know why. I don't know. We were only trying to find some plausible explanation of the murder."

I insisted. "Yeah, but how could you figure Eric Hagh? If she had lived a week longer he would still have his document and she would have a lot more property for him to claim half of."

"One possibility," Viola Duday suggested, "would be that she had denied that she had signed the document, or he thought she was going to, and he was afraid he would get nothing at all."

"But she had stated that she had signed the document."

"Had she? To whom?"

I couldn't very well say to Nero Wolfe and me, so I went official on her. "I'm asking the questions, Miss Duday. As I said, this is only preliminary, so I'll cover the rest of you on the routine." I focused on Daphne. "Miss O'Neil, how did you spend your time last night between ten-thirty and two o'clock? You understand that—"

There was the sound of a door opening behind me, the one by which I had entered, and I turned my head to see. Three men were filing in, one of whom, the one in front, I knew only too well. Seeing me, he stopped, gawked, and said right from his heart, "Well, by God!"

There has never been a time when the sight of Lieutenant Rowcliff of Manhattan

80

Homicide has done me good. Circumstances under which the sight of Rowcliff would do me good are not remotely imaginable. But if I had been keeping a list of the moments for him not to appear, that one would have been at the top, and there he was.

"You're under arrest," he said, nearly choking on it.

I controlled the impulse I always have when he comes in view, and which I will not describe. "In writing?" I inquired.

"I don't need any writing. I'm taking—" He checked himself, advanced to my elbow, and looked at the Softdown quintet. "Which one of you is Jay L. Brucker?"

"I am."

"I'm Lieutenant George Rowcliff of the Police Department. Downstairs this man said he was a policeman. Did he—"

"Isn't he?" Brucker demanded.

"No. Did he—"

"We're a pack of fools," Miss Duday snapped. "He's a reporter!"

Rowcliff raised his voice a notch. "He's no reporter. His name is Archie Goodwin, and he's the confidential assistant of Nero Wolfe, the private detective. Did he say he was a policeman?"

Three of them said yes. He shifted his

81

fishy popeyes to me. "I'm taking you in the act of impersonating an officer of the law, which is a felony and justifies severity. Handcuff him and search him, Doyle."

His two colleagues came toward me. I thrust my hands deep in my pants pocket, slumped, and slid forward in my chair, so that more than half of me was beneath the table. To frisk and cuff a 180-pound man relaxed in that position takes a determined attitude and plenty of muscle, and I was sure that the colleagues would halt at least to take a breath.

"You may remember," I told Rowcliff, "that on April third, nineteen forty-nine, by order of Commissioner Skinner, you signed a written apology to Mr. Wolfe and me. This one will be only to me, if I decide to accept one instead of hanging it on you."

"I'm taking you in the act."

"You are not. These people are nervous. Both downstairs and up here I identified myself with just two words, my name and the word 'detective,' and I showed my license, which no one took the trouble to examine. I didn't say I was a policeman. I am a detective, and I said so. I asked questions, and they answered. Apologize now and get it over with."

"What were you asking questions about?"

"Matters connected with the death of Priscilla Eads."

"About a homicide."

I conceded it. "Yes."

"Why?"

"As an interested citizen."

"What kind of interest? You lied to Inspector Cramer. You told him that Wolfe had no client, but here you are."

"It wasn't a lie. He had no client."

"Then he's got one since?"

"No. He has none."

"Then what are you here for? What kind of interest?"

"My own. I am interested for personal reasons, and Mr. Wolfe has nothing to do with it. I'm strictly on my own."

"For God's sake." From the tone of Rowcliff's voice, he had reached the limit of exasperated disgust. From my slumped position I couldn't see his face, but from a corner of my eye I had a view of his hand tightened into a fist. "So Wolfe *has* got a c-c-client." When he reached a certain pitch of excitement he was apt to stutter. I usually tried to beat him to it, but this time missed the chance. "And a client he doesn't dare to acknowledge. And you actually have the gall to try to cover for him by telling another outrageous lie, that you're here on your own. Your insolence—"

"Look, Lieutenant." I was earnest. "It has always been a pleasure to lie to you, and will be again, but I want to make it clear and emphatic that my interest in this case is strictly personal, as I said, and Mr. Wolfe is not concerned. If you—"

"That's enough." The fist was tighter and was quivering a little. Some day it would be too much for him and he would let fly, and my reaction would depend on the context. It couldn't be taken for granted that I would break him in two. He went on. "It's more than enough. Giving false information, withholding evidence, material witness, obstructing justice, and impersonating an officer of the law. Take him, Doyle. There'll be someone here soon to t-t-t-turn him over to."

He meant it. I considered swiftly. In spite of the current situation, I hoped and expected to have further dealings with some or all of the Softdown quintet, and it wouldn't help any to have them sit and watch while a pair of bozos dragged me from under a table, unavoidably mussing me up. So I arose, sidled around to the back of my chair, and told Doyle, "Please be careful. I'm ticklish."

—6—

At a quarter to six that afternoon I sat on a chair in a smallish room in a well-known building on Leonard Street. I was bored, disillusioned, and hungry. If I had known what was going to happen in sixty seconds, at fourteen minutes to six, my outlook would have been quite different, but I didn't.

I had been bandied a good deal, though I had not yet been tossed in the coop or even charged. Escorted first to the Tenth Precinct on West Twentieth Street, where Cramer's office is, I had sat neglected for half an hour, at the end of which I was told that if I wanted to see Inspector Cramer I would have to be taken elsewhere. I had expressed no desire to see Cramer, but I was tired of sitting, and when one in uniform invited me to accompany him I did so. He conveyed me in a taxi to 240 Centre Street, took me up in an elevator, and gripped my arm on a long walk around halls, winding up at an alcove with a bench, where he told me to sit. He also sat. After a while I asked him who or what we were waiting for.

"Listen, bud," he demanded aggressively, "do I look like I know much?"

I hedged. "At first sight, no."

"Right. I don't know one single thing about anything. So don't ask me."

That seemed to settle it, and I sat. People, the assortment you expect and always get at 240 Centre Street, kept passing by along the corridor, both directions. I was at the point where I was shifting on the hard bench every thirty seconds instead of every two minutes when I saw a captain in uniform marching past and called to him. "Captain!"

He stopped, whirled, saw me, and approached.

"Captain," I said, "I appeal to you. My name is Archie Goodwin, Nine-fourteen West Thirty-fifth Street, which is Nero Wolfe's address. This officer must of course stick to me or I might escape. I appeal to you to send me a photographer. I want a picture of me in these things"—I lifted my manacled hands—"for evidence. A double-breasted ape named Rowcliff had me fettered, and I intend to sue him for false

86

arrest and exposing me to shame, degradation, and public scorn."

"I'll see what I can do," he said sympathetically and went.

I had of course stopped the captain and appealed to him as a diversion, just for something to do, and it was totally unexpected when, some twenty minutes later, a sergeant walked up to me and asked my name. I told him.

He turned to my chaperon. "What's this man's name?"

"He told you, Sergeant."

"I'm asking you!"

"I don't know of my own knowledge, Sergeant. Up at Homicide they said his name was Archie Goodwin, like he told you."

The sergeant made a noise, not complimentary, glanced at my cuffs, produced a ring of keys and used one, and my hands were free. I had never seen that captain before and haven't seen him since, and I don't know his name, but if you ever get stuck in an alcove at headquarters with handcuffs on, ask for a captain around fifty to fifty-five with a big red nose and a double chin, wearing metal-rimmed glasses.

A little later another sergeant came with orders, and I was escorted down and out, to

Leonard Street, up to the District Attorney's layout, and to a room. There at last some attention was paid to me, by a Homicide dick named Randall, whom I knew a little, and an assistant DA I had never seen before, named Mandelbaum. They pecked at me for an hour and a half, and there was nothing in it for anybody, except that I got the impression that there would be no charge. When they left they didn't even bother about a sentinel, merely telling me to stick. The third or fourth time I looked at my watch after their departure it was a quarter to six.

As I said, I was bored and disillusioned and hungry. An encounter with Rowcliff was enough to ruin a day anyhow, and that was only one item of the record. I had to meet Lon Cohen at seven-thirty to buy him a steak as promised, and afterward I had to go home and pack a bag before finding a hotel room. That was okay, but there was no telling what frame of mind they had pestered Wolfe into, and if I went home he would probably be laying for me. Also I didn't mind sleeping in a hotel room, but what about when I left it in the morning? What were my plans? I shrugged that off, thinking I would get some kind of lead from

Lon, and decided to call him then instead of waiting until seven. There was no phone in the room where I was, so I got up and went out to the corridor, glanced right and left, and started left. There were doors on both sides, all closed. I preferred one standing open, with a phone in sight, and kept going. No luck. But nearly at the end of the corridor the last door on the left was ajar, a three-inch crack, and as I approached it I heard a voice. That was the event I have referred to as occurring at fourteen minutes to six—my hearing that voice, coming from that room. At twelve paces it was audible, at five paces it was recognizable, and when I got my ear within six inches of the crack the words were quite plain.

"This whole performance," Nero Wolfe was saying, "is based on an idiotic assumption, which was natural and indeed inevitable, since Mr. Rowcliff is your champion ass—the assumption that Mr. Goodwin and I are both cretins. I do not deny that at times in the past I have been less than candid with you—I will acknowledge, to humor you, that I have humbugged and hoodwinked to serve my purpose—but I still have my license, and you know what that means. It means that on balance I have helped you more than I have hurt you—not the community, which is another matter, but you, Mr. Cramer, and you, Mr. Bowen, and of course you others too."

So the DA himself was in the audience.

"It means also that I have known where to stop, and Mr. Goodwin has too. That is our unbroken record, and you know it. But what happens today? Following my customary routine, at four o'clock this afternoon I go up to my plant rooms for two hours of relaxation. I have been there but a short time when I hear a commotion and go to investigate. It is Mr. Rowcliff. He has taken advantage of the absence of Mr. Goodwin, whom he fears and petulantly envies, and has entered my house by force and—"

"That's a lie!" Rowcliff's voice came. "I rang and—"

"Shut up!" Wolfe roared, and it seemed to me that the door moved to narrow the crack a little. In a moment he went on, not roaring but not whispering either, "As you all know, a policeman has no more right to enter a man's home than anyone else, except under certain adequately defined circumstances. But such a right is often usurped, as today when my cook and housekeeper unlatched the door and Mr. Rowcliff pushed it open against resistance, entered, brushed my employee aside, and ignored all protests while he was illegally mounting three flights of stairs, erupting into my plant rooms, and invading my privacy."

I leaned against the jamb and got comfortable.

"He was ass enough to suppose I would speak with him. Naturally I ordered him out. He insisted that I must answer questions. When I persisted in my refusal and turned to leave him, he intercepted me, displayed a warrant for my arrest as a material witness in a murder case, and put a hand on me." The voice suddenly went lower and much colder. "I will not have a hand put on me, gentlemen. I like no man's hand on me, and one such as Mr. Rowcliff's, unmerited, I will not have. I told him to give me his instructions under the authority of the warrant, in as few words as possible, without touching me. I am not bragging of my extreme sensitiveness to hostile touch, since it is shared by all the animals; I mention it only as one of the reasons why I refused to speak to Mr. Rowcliff. He took me into custody under the warrant, conducted me out of my house, and, in a rickety old police car with a headstrong and paroxysmal driver, brought me to this building."

I bit my lip. While the fact that he too had been arrested and bandied was not without its charm, the additional fact that I was responsible made it nothing to titter about. Therefore I did not titter. I listened.

"I had assumed, charitably, that some major misapprehension, possibly even excusable, had driven Mr. Rowcliff to this frenzied zeal. But I learned from you, Mr. Bowen, that it was merely an insane fit of nincompoopery. To accuse Mr. Goodwin of impersonating a policeman is infantile; I don't know what he said or did, and I don't need to; I know Mr. Goodwin, and he couldn't possibly be so fatuous. To accuse him, acting on my account, of giving false information may not be infantile, but it is pointless. You suspect that I have been hired by someone involved, either innocently or guiltily, in the death of Miss Eads and Mrs. Fomos, that I wish to conceal that fact, and that Mr. Goodwin went to that place today as my agent and, denying it, is lying."

"I know damn well he is," a voice blurted—Rowcliff's.

"The arrangement," Wolfe said curtly, "was that I was to speak without interruption. I say the accusation is pointless. If Mr. Goodwin is lying on instruction from me, do you suppose I didn't consider the probabilities? Is it likely that I'll be halted or deflected by such inanities as putting handcuffs on him—yes, Mr. Rowcliff actually flaunted that—or dragging me down here in an unsafe vehicle? You suspect that I have a client; that I know something you don't know and would like to; and that you can bully it out of me. You can't, because I haven't got it. But you're correct in thinking I have a client. I admit it. I have."

Rowcliff's voice ejaculated something that sounded like a cry of triumph. I thought to myself, At last here it is. The sonofagun has got himself a customer!

Wolfe was going on. "I didn't have a client this morning, or even an hour ago, but now I have. Mr. Rowcliff's ferocious spasms, countenanced by you gentlemen, have made the challenge ineluctable. When Mr. Goodwin said that I was not concerned in this matter and that he was acting solely in his own personal interest, he was telling the truth. As you may know, he is not indifferent to those attributes of young women that constitute the chief reliance of our race in our gallant struggle against the menace of the insects. He is especially vulnerable to young women who possess not only those more obvious charms but also have a knack of stimulating his love of chivalry and adventure and his preoccupation with the picturesque and the passionate. Priscilla Eads was such a woman. She spent some time with Mr. Goodwin yesterday; he locked her in a bedroom of my house. Within three hours of her eviction by him at my behest, she was brutally murdered. I will not say that the effect on him amounted to derangement, but it was considerable. He bounded out of my house like a man obsessed, after telling me that he was going single-handed after a murderer, and after arming himself. It was pathetic, but it was also humane, romantic, and thoroughly admirable, and your callous and churlish treatment of him leaves me with no alternative. I am at his service. He is my client."

Rowcliff's voice blurted incredulously, "You mean *Archie Goodwin* is your client?"

The dry cutting voice of Bowen, the DA, put in, "All that rigmarole was leading up to *that?*"

I pushed the door open and stepped in.

Eight pairs of eyes came at me. Besides Wolfe, Bowen, Cramer, and Rowcliff, there were the two who had been pecking at me previously, and two others, strangers. I crossed toward Wolfe. It had been desirable to let him know that I had heard what he said before witnesses, but it was equally desirable to make it plain that his new client had the warmest appreciation of the honor.

"I'm hungry," I told him. "I had a soda-fountain lunch and I could eat a porcupine with quills on. Let's go home."

His reaction was humane, romantic, and thoroughly admirable. As if we had re-hearsed it a dozen times, he arose without a word, got his hat and stick from a nearby table, came and gave me a pat on the shoul-der, growled at the audience, "A paradise for puerility," and turned and headed for the door. I followed. No one moved to in-tercept us.

Since I knew the building better than he did, I took the lead in the corridor and got us downstairs and out to the street. In the taxi he sat with his lips pressed tight, grip-ping the strap. There was no conversation. At the curb in front of home I paid the driver, got out and held the door for him, preceded him up the stoop, and used my key, but the key was not enough. The door opened an inch and was stopped by the chain bolt, so I had to ring for Fritz. After he had come and let us in, Wolfe instructed us, "Never again an unbolted door. Never!" To Fritz: "You proceeded with the kidney?"

"Yes, sir. You didn't phone."

"The dumplings and burnt sugar?"

"Yes, sir."

"Satisfactory. Beer, please. I'm so dry I crackle."

His hat and stick disposed of, he went to the office, and I tagged. For hours I had been sweaty where the leather holster kept my skin from breathing, and it was a relief to get rid of the thing. That attended to, I did not sit at my desk. Instead I went to the red leather chair—the chair where a thousand clients had sat, not to mention thousands who had never attained cliency. I lowered myself into it, leaned back, and crossed my legs. Fritz came with beer, and Wolfe opened, poured, and drank.

He looked at me. "Buffoon," he stated.

I shook my head. "No, sir. I sit here not as a gag but to avoid misunderstanding. As a client, the closer to you the better. As an employee, nothing doing until my personal problem is solved. If you meant what you said down there, tell me how much you want for a retainer, and I'll give you a check.

If not, all I can do is bound out of your house like a man obsessed."

"Confound it, I'm helpless! I'm committed!"

"Yes, sir. How about a retainer?"

"No!"

"Would you care to hear how I spent the day?"

"Care to? No. But how the devil can I escape it?"

I reported in full. Gradually, as he progressed to his third glass of beer and on through it, the wrinkles of his scowl smoothed out some. Apparently he was paying no attention to me, but I had long ago learned not to worry about that. It would all be available any time he needed it. When I finished he grunted.

"How many of those five people could you have here at eleven in the morning?"

"As it stands now? With no more bait?"

"Yes."

"I wouldn't bet on one, but I'm ready to try. I might get something useful from Lon Cohen if I buy him a thick enough steak—and by the way, I ought to call him."

"Do so. Invite him to dine with us."

On the face of it that suggestion was gracious and generous, and maybe it was, but the situation was complicated. If we had been engaged on the case in the usual manner, and, after dope, I had taken Lon to Pierre's for a feed, it would of course have gone on the expense account and we would have been reimbursed. But this was different. If I listed it as an expense Wolfe was stuck unless he billed me as a client. If I didn't list it I was stuck and there could be no deduction on an income-tax report, either Wolfe's or mine, which wouldn't do at all.

So I phoned Lon, and he came and ate kidneys mountain style, and carameled dumplings, instead of a Pierre steak, which was convenient and economical but had its drawback—namely, that I usually dispose of six of those dumplings and this time was limited to four; and Wolfe had to be content with seven instead of ten. He took it like a man, filling the gap with an extra helping of salad and cheese.

Back in the office after dinner, I had to hand it to Lon. He was full of food as good as a man can hope for anywhere, and wine to go with it, but he was not blurry. My phoning him twice and the invitation to dine had him set either to take or to give, whichever was on the program, and as he relaxed in one of the yellow chairs, sipping B & B, his eyes darted from Wolfe to me and back again.

Wolfe's chest billowed with a deep sigh. "I'm in a pickle, Mr. Cohen," he declared. "I am committed to investigate a murder and I have no entree. When Archie told you today that I was not interested in the death of Miss Eads it was a truth, but now I am, and I need a toehold. Who killed her?"

Lon shook his head. "I was intending to ask you. Of course you know it's out that she was here yesterday, that she left here not long before she was killed, so everybody takes it for granted that you're working on it. Since when have you needed an entree?"

Wolfe squinted at him. "Are you in my debt, Mr. Cohen, or am I in yours?"

"I'll call it square if you will."

"Good. Then I assume I have credit. I'll read your paper in the morning, and others too, but here we are now. Do you mind talking about it?"

Lon said he didn't mind a bit and proceeded to prove it. He talked for nearly an hour, with some questions from Wolfe and a few from me, and when he finished we may have been better informed but had nothing you could call an entree.

Helmar, Brucker, Quest, Pitkin, and Miss Duday would not only own eighty per cent of the Softdown stock; they would also be in control of the distribution of another ten per cent of it to employees, with power to decide who got what. That made up the ninety per cent disposed of under the will of Priscilla's father. The remaining ten per cent had been owned by an associate in the business, deceased, and now belonged to his daughter, a Mrs. Sarah Jaffee, a widow. Mrs. Jaffee had formerly been a close friend of Priscilla Eads. Her husband had been killed a year ago in Korea.

The favorite suspect with male journalists was Oliver Pitkin, for no convincing reason; the favorite with females was Viola Duday. No evidence had been disclosed that any of the five main beneficiaries was in financial difficulties or was excessively rancorous, greedy, or bloodthirsty; but since each of them would get an engraved certificate worth roughly a million and a half, the consensus was that such evidence was not required. As far as the press knew, none of them was eliminated by alibi or other circumstance. Of some sixty reporters, from all papers and wire services, working on the case, at least half were certain that Daphne O'Neil was deeply involved one way or another, and were determined to find out how.

The news that Priscilla had spent seven of her last hours on earth at Wolfe's house had come through Perry Helmar, who had got it from an assistant DA. Helmar had told an AP City News man in the middle of the afternoon, and an hour later, refusing to see reporters, had issued a statement regarding his own visit to Wolfe and the "cruel deception" that had been practiced on him. The statement had been carried by the evening papers. It did not say, but clearly implied, that if Wolfe had not concealed from Helmar the presence of Priscilla in his house she would not have been killed. Lon's paper, the *Gazette*, would give it a box on page three. When Lon mentioned that detail he paused and cocked his head at Wolfe, inviting comment, but got none.

Priscilla Eads' life had been complicated by a series of phases she had gone through. After her father's death when she was fifteen, her home had been with the Helmars, but she had spent most of the time away at school, where she had made a brilliant record, including two years at Smith. Then suddenly, a few months before her nineteenth birthday, she had quit in the middle of a semester, announced to friends that she intended to see the world, rented an apartment in Greenwich Village, hired a maid and cook and butler, and started giving parties. In a few months she had had enough of the Village, but Lon's information on her next move was a little vague. The way a *Gazette* man had got it, her maid had decided she must go to New Orleans to see her sick mother, and Priscilla, glad of any excuse to get away from the Village, and particularly from her guardian, Perry Helmar, who was pestering her to return to college, bought plane tickets to New Orleans for herself and her maid, and off they went.

Probably in New Orleans, but anyhow somewhere around there, she had met Eric Hagh. On this Lon was even vaguer, but it was definite that she had met him, married him, and gone off with him to some part of South America where he had something to do with something. It was also definite that three months later she had suddenly appeared in New York, accompanied by the maid she had gone away with, but not by a husband; bought a house in the woods not far from Mount Kisco; and started in on men. For two years she had raised some miscellaneous hell with men, apparently with the idea that the higher you jacked up an expectation the more fun it was to watch it crash when you jerked it loose. In time that lost its appeal, and she moved to Reno, stayed the prescribed time, got her divorce, returned to New York, and joined the Salvation Army.

At that detail I had given Lon a stare, thinking that surely he had pulled it out of a hat. Priscilla Eads as I had known her, in the peach-colored dress and tailored jacket, was mighty hard to picture as a consecrated tambourine shaker. But obviously Lon was dealing it straight, with no fancy touches for effect.

Priscilla had actually stuck with the Salvation Army for nearly two years, in uniform, working seven days a week, giving up all her old friends and habits, and living modestly if not frugally. Then abruptly—she had always been abrupt—she had quit the Army, moved to a duplex apartment on East Seventy-fourth Street, and begun to take an active interest, for the first time, in the affairs of Softdown, Incorporated. That had aroused feelings in various quarters. It was known that there had been friction between her and her former guardian, Perry Helmar, still the trustee of the property soon to become hers. Specifically, it was known that some months ago she had fired Daphne O'Neil, told her to leave the premises and not come back, and had been overruled by the officers of the corporation, supported by Helmar, who was legally in control. There was no record of any threat or mortal attack.

The events of Monday night were pretty well timetabled. According to the driver of the taxi I had put Priscilla into, she had told him to take her to Grand Central Station. Arrived there, she said she had changed her mind; she wanted to ride around Central Park. He obliged. When, after a leisurely winding trip clear to the north end and back down to Central Park South, she had said she was thinking something over and wanted to do another lap, he had got prudent and mentioned money, and she had handed him a ten. When they were completing the second circuit, she gave him an address, 618 East Seventy-fourth Street, and he drove her there, arriving shortly after one o'clock. He helped her with the luggage, out of the cab and through the entrance door, which she opened with her key, and then returned to his cab and drove off.

It was generally believed, by both the

cops and the press, that the murderer had been in her apartment waiting for her, and that he had got in with the key which the maid, Margaret Fomos, had in her bag. So he had already killed Margaret Fomos to get the bag, not necessarily planning it that way. He might have counted on getting it at smaller cost but had been recognized by her; and she, having been with Priscilla for years, could have recognized anyone who had known Priscilla well.

I filled half a notebook with the stuff Lon Cohen gave us that evening, but I guess the above samples will do for this record. After escorting him to the front, I returned to the office and found Wolfe with his chin on his chest and his eyes closed. Not opening them, he asked what time it was, and I told him ten-thirty.

He grunted. "Too late to expect a welcome from people. What time is it in Venezuela?"

"My God, I don't know."

I started to cross to the big globe over by the bookshelves, but he beat me to it. Anything for an excuse to consult the globe. He ran his finger along a meridian, starting at Quebec and ending at the equator. "Several degrees east. An hour later, I suppose." He twirled the globe, looking disappointed.

I thought it was pure fake and I resented it. "You're right near the Panama Canal," I suggested. "Go on through to the other ocean. Try Galápagos. It's only half-past nine there."

He ignored it. "Get your notebook," he growled. "If I'm saddled with this thing, I am. Your program for the morning."

I obeyed.

—7—

Probably my conception of a widow was formed in my early boyhood in Ohio, from a character called Widow Rowley, who lived across the street. I have known others since, but the conception has not been entirely obliterated, so there is always an element of shock when I meet a female who has been labeled widow and I find that she has some teeth, does not constantly mutter to herself, and can walk without a cane.

Mrs. Sarah Jaffee was not visibly burdened with any handicaps whatever. She was probably more than one-third the age of Widow Rowley had been, but not much.

That much, along with the shock, took only one good glance as she admitted me to her sixth-floor apartment on East Eightieth Street, and the glance also furnished another mild shock. Although it was ten in the morning of a pleasant and sunny June day, there in her foyer was a man's topcoat thrown carelessly over the back of a chair, and on a polished tabletop was a man's felt hat. I kept my brows down, merely remarking to myself, as she led me through a large and luxurious living room, that since I had phoned for permission to come, and so was expected, it might have been supposed that a widow would have taken the trouble to tidy up a little.

When, beyond the living room, we came upon a table in an alcove with breakfast tools in place for two, I will not say that I blushed, but I felt that I had not been properly briefed.

"I was in bed when you phoned," she said, sitting and picking up a spoon. "I assume you've had breakfast, but how about some coffee? Sit down—no, not there, that's my husband's place. Olga! A coffee cup, please!"

A door swung open and a Valkyrie entered with a cup and saucer in her hand.

"On a tray, my pet," Mrs. Jaffee said, and the Valkyrie whirled and disappeared. Before the door had stopped swinging she breezed in again with cup and saucer on a tray, and I backstepped not to get trampled. When she had gone I got my coffee from my hostess and went to a chair on the other side. She took her spoon and scooped a bite of melon.

"It's all right," she said, reassuring me. "I'm a nut, that's all." She opened wide for the bite of melon, and there was no question about her having teeth, very nice ones. I took a sip of coffee, which was barely drinkable for a man used to Fritz's.

"You know my husband is dead," she stated.

I nodded. "So I understood."

She took another bite of melon and disposed of it. "He was in the Reserve, a major, a Signal Corps technician. When he went away, one day in March a year ago, he left his hat and coat there in the hall. I didn't put them away. When I got word he had been killed, three months later, they were still there. That was a year ago, and there they are, and I'm sick of looking at them, I'm simply sick to death of looking at them, but there they are."

She pointed. "There's his breakfast place too, and I'm sick of looking at that. Weren't you surprised when I told you on the phone, all right, come ahead? You, a complete stranger, a detective wanting to ask me questions about a murder?"

"A little, maybe," I conceded, not to be cranky.

"Of course you were." She dropped a slice of bread into the slot of the toaster and spooned another bite of melon. "But at that I lost my nerve. A while back I decided to quit being a nut, and I decided the way I would do it—I would have a man do it for me. I would have a man sit here with me at breakfast, in Dick's place—my husband's place—and I would have him take that awful hat and coat out of that hall. But do you know what?"

I said I didn't.

She finished the melon, popped the toast out, and started putting butter on it before telling me what. "There wasn't a man I could ask! Out of all the men I know, there wasn't one that would have understood! But I was determined it had to be done that way, so there I was. And this morning, when you phoned, I was all shaky anyway, it was so horrible about Pris, the way she died, and I thought to myself, This man's a stranger, it doesn't matter whether he understands or not, he can sit and eat breakfast with me and he can take that coat and hat out of there."

She turned her palms up and made a face. "And did you hear me?" She mimicked herself. " 'I assume you've had breakfast—no, not there, that's my husband's place.' I just simply lost my nerve. Do you suppose I really am a nut?"

I arose, circled the end of the table, sat in the chair at her right, took the napkin, picked up the plate and extended my arm, and demanded, "That piece of toast, please?"

She goggled at me a full three seconds before she moved a hand for the toast, slow motion. The hand was quite steady.

"Excuse me," I said, "but I suppose I ought to eat it if you want this to stick, and it's that godawful cellophane special, so if there's any jelly or marmalade or honey . . ."

She got up and left through the swinging door. In a little she was back with an assortment of jars on a tray. I selected one that was labeled plum jam and helped myself. She made another piece of toast, buttered it and took a bite, and poured more coffee for us. She ate the last crumb of toast before she spoke. "If you hadn't been rude about the bread I would soon have been crying."

"Yeah, I thought so."

"Will you take that coat and hat away with you?"

"Certainly."

She was frowning at me. She put out a hand as if to touch my arm, then withdrew it. "Do you mean to say you understand?"

"Gosh, no, I'm just a stranger." I pushed my coffee cup back. "Look, Mrs. Jaffee, it's like this. Nero Wolfe is investigating the murder of Priscilla Eads for a client. As I told you on the phone, we have no idea that you know anything at all about the murder, directly or indirectly, but you may have information that will help. You inherited from your father ten per cent of the stock of Softdown, Incorporated, and for a time you were Priscilla Eads' closest friend. Isn't that right?"

"Yes."

"When did you see her last?"

She used her napkin on lips and fingers, dropped it on the table, pushed back her chair, and arose. "We'll be more comfortable in the other room," she said, and

111

moved. I followed, through to the living room, where it was cooler, with the slanted venetian blinds admitting only a dim and restful light. The furniture was all wearing light blue slipcovers that looked as if none of them had been sat on yet. After she had got cigarettes from an enameled box and I had lit them, she perched with cushions on an oversized divan, looking less than ever like Widow Rowley, and I took a chair.

"You know," she said, "my mind is a very funny thing. I guess there's no doubt I'm a nut. When you asked me just now about seeing Pris, when I saw her last, I realized for the first time that someone did it."

"Did what? Killed her?"

She nodded. "I didn't hear about it until late yesterday afternoon, when a friend told me on the phone. I never see an evening paper, and I haven't looked at this morning's paper yet, and anyhow I probably wouldn't read about it because I can't stand things like that. I seem to just shut my eyes to things I can't stand. So I knew Pris was dead, found dead in her apartment, strangled, but that was all. When you asked me when I saw her last, it hit me all of a sudden that someone actually *did it!* She didn't do it herself, did she?"

"Not unless somebody helped out by removing the cord for her afterward. She was strangled with some kind of cord."

Mrs. Jaffee shivered and seemed to shrink into the cushions. "Did that—would that take long?"

"Probably not."

"How long?"

"If the cord was good and tight, only a few seconds until she lost consciousness."

Her hands were fists, and I suspected that the sharp nails were marking her palms. "What could a woman do if a man was strangling her with a cord and had it pulled tight?"

"Nothing except die if he meant business." I got gruff. "You're taking it too hard. If I had started strangling you when you started feeling it a minute ago, it would be all over by now." I reached to mash the cigarette she had dropped into the tray. "Let's go back and try again. When did you see Miss Eads last?"

She took a long deep breath with her lips parted, and her fists loosened some. "I don't think I want to talk about it."

"That's just fine." I was indignant. "You owe me three dollars."

"What? What for?"

"Taxi fare here to take your husband's place at breakfast, which was why you let me come. It will be more going back because I'll have to stop at the Salvation Army to get rid of the hat and coat I promised to take. Three bucks will cover it, and I prefer cash."

She shook her head, frowning at me. "Have I ever met you before?"

"Not that I remember, and I think I would. Why?"

"You seem to know exactly the right things to say, as if you knew all about me. What day's today?"

"Wednesday."

"Then the last time I saw Pris was one week ago today, last Wednesday. She phoned and asked me to have lunch with her, and I did. She wanted to know if I would come to a special meeting of Softdown stockholders on July first, the day after her twenty-fifth birthday."

"Did you say you would?"

"No. That's another way my mind is funny. Since my father died, seven years ago, and left me twelve thousand shares of

114

Softdown stock, I have never gone near the place, for meetings or anything else. I get a very good income from it, but I don't know one single thing about it. Have you met a man named Perry Helmar?"

I said I had.

"Well, he's been after me for years to come to meetings, but I wouldn't, because I was afraid that if I did something would happen to the business that would reduce my income, and it would be my fault. Why should I run a risk like that when all I had to do was stay away? Do you know any of those people down there—Brucker and Quest and Pitkin and that Viola Duday?"

I said I did.

"Well, they've been after me too, every one of them at different times, to give them a proxy to vote my stock at a meeting, and I wouldn't do that either. I didn't—"

"You mean give them a proxy jointly—all of them?"

"Oh, no, separately. They've been after me one at a time, but the worst was that woman Duday. Isn't she a terror?"

"I guess so. I don't know her as well as you do. Why did Miss Eads want you at a special stockholders meeting?"

"She said she wanted to elect a new board

of directors, and it would be all women, and they would elect Viola Duday president of the corporation—that's right, isn't it, president of the corporation?"

"It sounds like it. Did she say who would be on the new board of directors?"

"Yes, but I don't—wait, maybe I do. She and I were to be—Pris and I—and Viola Duday, and some woman in charge of something at the factory—I forget her name—and Pris's maid, the one that's been with her for so long—her name's Margaret, but I forget her last name."

I supplied it. "Fomos. Margaret Fomos."

"No, that's not—oh, yes, of course. She's been married."

I nodded. "She has also been killed. She was waylaid on the street and strangled to death Monday night, a couple of hours before Priscilla Eads."

Sarah Jaffee's eyes popped. "Margaret has—too?"

"Yes. Was that all, those five, to be—"

"She was strangled just like Pris?"

"Yes. Apparently the idea was to get a key to Miss Eads' apartment, since there was a key in the maid's bag and the bag was taken. Were they to make up the new board of directors, those five women?"

"Yes."

"But you told her you wouldn't go to the meeting?"

Mrs. Jaffee's hands were fists again, but not as tight as before. "And I told her I wouldn't be a director either. I didn't want to get mixed up in it in any way at all. I didn't want to have anything whatever to do with it. She said I seemed to be perfectly willing to accept the dividend checks, and I said certainly I was and I hoped they would keep coming forever, and they probably wouldn't if I started butting in. I told her I hoped her new arrangement, the board of directors and the president, would work all right, but if it didn't there was nothing I could do about it."

"Had she asked you before about coming to a stockholders' meeting?"

"No, that was the first time. I hadn't seen her for more than a year. She phoned and came to see me when she heard about Dick's—my husband's—death."

"I thought she was your closest friend."

"Oh, that was a long time ago."

"How long?"

She eyed me. "I'm not enjoying this a bit."

"I know you're not."

"It's not doing anyone any good either."

"It might. However. I figure I've got a dollar's worth, so I'll settle for two bucks if you insist."

She turned her head and called, "Olga!" In a moment the Valkyrie came marching in, by no means silently. Mrs. Jaffee asked her if there was any coffee left, and she said there was and was requested to bring some. She went and soon was back with the order, this time on a tray without being told. Mrs. Jaffee wriggled to the edge of the divan, poured, and sipped.

"I can tell you how old I was," she said, "when I first met Pris."

I said I would appreciate it very much.

She sipped more coffee. "I was four years old. Pris was about two weeks. My father was in her father's business, and the families were friends. Of course, with children four years is a big difference, but we liked each other all along, and when Pris's mother died, and soon afterward her father, and Pris went to live with the Helmars, she and I got to be like sisters. We were apart a lot, since we went to different schools, and I graduated from college the year she started, but we wrote to each other—we must have written a thousand letters back and forth. Do you know about her leaving college and setting up a menage in the Village?"

I said I did.

"That was when we were closest. My father had died then, and my mother long before, and I practically lived with Pris, though I had a little place of my own. The trouble with Pris is she has too much money."

"Was and had," I corrected.

"Oh. Yes. Her income was enormous. After a few months of the Village all of a sudden she was off, and do you know what her excuse was? Her maid—that was Margaret—she had to take Margaret to New Orleans to see her sick mother! Did you ever hear anything to beat it? Off she went, leaving me to close up the place in the Village. We were still friends all right; she wrote me from New Orleans raving about it, and the first thing I knew, here came a letter saying that she had found her prince and married him, and they were off for Peru, where he had an option on the Andes Mountains, or approximately that."

Mrs. Jaffee finished the coffee, put the cup and saucer down on the tray, and wriggled back until she was against the cushions. "That," she said, "was the last letter I

119

ever got from Pris. The very last. Maybe I still have it—I remember she enclosed a picture of him. I wondered why she didn't write, and then one day she phoned me—she was back in New York, and she was alone, except for Margaret, and she was calling herself Miss Priscilla Eads. I saw her a few times, and when she bought a place up in Westchester I went there once, but she was a completely different person, and she didn't invite me again, and I wouldn't have gone if she had. For nearly three years I didn't see her at all, until she had been to Reno and come back and joined the Salvation Army—do you know about that?"

I said yes.

"She was through with that too at the time she heard of my husband's death and came to see me. She had decided to take up her father's business where he had left off, only of course she wouldn't own it until she was twenty-five. She seemed more like the old Pris, and we might have got together again, but I had just lost Dick and I was in no condition to get together with anyone, so, the way it went, I didn't see her again until last week, and then I didn't—"

She stopped abruptly and jerked her chin up. "For God's sake, my not doing what she wanted—that didn't have anything to do with her being killed, did it? Is that why you wanted to see me?"

I shook my head. "I can't answer the first one, but it's not why I wanted to see you. Did she get in touch with you again? A phone call or letter?"

"No."

"Did any of the others, the Softdown people?"

"No."

"Where were you Monday night? Not that I want an affidavit, but the police will be asking."

"They will not!"

"Sure they will, unless they crack it before they get to you. Practice on me. Name the people you were playing Canasta with."

"I wasn't. I was at home. Here."

"Any company? Or was Olga here?"

"No."

I shrugged. "That requires no practice." I leaned to her a little. "Look, Mrs. Jaffee, I might as well admit it. I'm here under false pretenses. I said we wanted information, Mr. Wolfe and I, and we do, but we also want help. Of course you know of the provisions of Priscilla's father will? Now that she is dead, you know that five people—

Helmar, Brucker, Quest, Pitkin, and Miss Duday—you know that they will own most of the Softdown stock?"

"Yes, certainly." She was frowning, concentrating at me.

"Okay. You're a stockholder. We want you to bring an action against those five people. Use your own lawyer, or we'll recommend one. We want you to ask a court for an injunction restraining them from exercising any of the rights of ownership of that stock until it is determined whether one or more of them acquired it by the commission of a crime. We think that under the circumstances a court will entertain such a request and may grant it."

"But what—" Her frown was deeper. "Why should I do that?"

"Because you have a legitimate interest in the proper handling of the firm's affairs. Because you were Priscilla's oldest friend, and formerly her closest one. Who do you think killed her?"

"I don't know. I wish you—don't do this!"

"This is what I came for. It may amount to nothing. The police may get it fast, today or tomorrow, and if so that settles it. But they may never get it, that has been known to happen, and a week or a month from now may be too late for Mr. Wolfe to start on it, and anyhow his client won't wait. We can't march in as the cops can. We have to have some way of getting at those people, we have to get a foot in, and this will do it. I'll tell you, Mrs. Jaffee, I'm not going to contribute any cracks about your accepting dividend checks, but it is true that that business has been supporting you in pretty good style for a long time, and this isn't much for it to ask in return, especially since you can be darned sure Priscilla Eads would be asking it too if she could talk. It won't take—"

I stopped because only a sap goes on talking to someone who is walking out on him. As she left the divan and started off she said nothing, but she sure was walking out. At an arch at the far end of the room she turned and spoke. "I won't do it! I won't do that!"

She was gone. A moment later the sound came of a door closing—not slamming, but firmly closing. After standing and considering a little, and deciding that I was out of ammunition for that target at that time and place, I moved in the opposite direction to the one she had taken, to the entrance foyer.

Crossing it, my eye caught the hat on the table and the coat on the back of the chair.

What the hell, I thought, and picked them up and took them along.

—8—

It was going on noon when, having made three stops en route, I paid off my hackie at the corner of Twenty-ninth and Lexington and walked east. The first stop had been at a drugstore to phone Wolfe and report lack of progress; the second had been at the Salvation Army depot to donate the coat and hat; and the third had been at the restaurant where, according to Lon Cohen, Andreas Fomos was employed as a waiter. Informed that Fomos was taking the day off, I had proceeded to his residence.

Not with any high expectations. My main hope had been to escort Sarah Jaffee to Thirty-fifth Street for a session with Wolfe and Nathaniel Parker, the only lawyer Wolfe has ever sent orchids to, arranging details about the injunction. Having flubbed that one, this stab at Fomos, as instructed by Wolfe, struck me as a damn poor substitute motion. So it was not with any enthusiasm for the errand, but merely as routine through long training, that as I approached the number on East Twenty-ninth Street I cased the area with a sharp and thorough eye, and, focusing on a spot across the street, recognized something. Crossing over, I entered a dingy and cluttered shoe-repair shop, and confronted a man seated there who, at my approach, had lifted a newspaper so as to hide his face from view.

I addressed the newspaper distinctly. "Get Lieutenant Rowcliff. I think I'm going to impersonate an officer of the law. I feel it coming."

The newspaper came down, disclosing the plump features, not quite puffy yet, of a city employee named Halloran. "You got good eyes," he said, just stating a fact. "If you mean disrespect for the lieutenant you mentioned, go right ahead."

"Some other time. Right now I'm working. I was glad to see you because I may be walking into a trap. If I don't come out in three days, phone Rowcliff. Is this a really serious tail, or are you on him alone?"

"I came in here for a pair of shoestrings."

I apologized for interrupting, left him, and headed across the street. Apparently Homicide had by no means wrapped it up, since they thought it necessary to keep an eye on Fomos, who, so far as I knew from what I had read in the papers, was involved only in that he had been bereaved; but surely Fomos wasn't really hot or I would have got a very different reaction from Halloran.

It was a five-story old red brick building. In the row of names under the mailboxes at the right of the vestibule, Fomos was next to the end. I pressed the button, waited half a minute for the click to come, pushed the door open, entered, and made for the stairs. There were three doors on each landing, one at each end and one in the middle. Three flights up, the one at the far end was sporting a big rosette of black ribbon with streamers hanging nearly to the floor. I went to it and pressed the button, and in a moment a gruff deep voice came at me through the wood. "Who is it?"

On the theory that I deserved to take a little something for an hour and a half's hard work, I called, "A friend of Sarah Jaffee's! My name's Goodwin!"

Abruptly the door popped open, wide open, and standing there was Hercules, in white shorts, dazzling white in contrast to his dark skin and his tousled mop of coal-black hair. "I'm in mourning," he said. "What do you want?"

"You're Andreas Fomos?"

"I'm Andy Fomos. No one says Andreas. What do you want?"

"I want to ask if you know why Priscilla Eads was going to make your wife a director of Softdown, Incorporated."

"What?" He cocked his head. "Say that again."

I repeated it. When he was sure he had it he turned his palms up. "Look," he rumbled. "I don't believe it."

"That's what Miss Eads told Mrs. Jaffee last week, that she was going to make your wife a director. A week ago today."

"I still don't believe it. Look. That Priscilla Eads was mixed up with some bad stars. She went crazy every two years. I have studied the history of it and I had it written down, but the police wanted it and I let them have it. I only met my wife and married her two years ago, but she told me the whole story. The Greenwich Village, the New Orleans, the Peru with a husband, the back here without him and getting even with men, the Reno, the Salvation Army!" His hands went up. "I ask you! My wife was with her through all that. Now you say

127

she was going to make my wife a director—did I say I don't believe it? Of course I believe it, why not? With that Priscilla Eads I could believe anything; but I don't know about it. What do you want?"

"We could talk better inside," I suggested, "if you don't mind."

"Are you a reporter?"

"No. I—"

"Are you a cop?"

"No. I work—"

I don't know how many hundreds of times people have undertaken to close doors on me, but often enough so that my reaction has become routine and automatic—in fact, too automatic. When Andy Fomos jerked aside and started swinging the door to, my foot went out as usual, ready to hold the floor against pressure as usual, but with him usual wasn't good enough. He was even faster and stronger than he looked, and instead of bringing his weight to it, which would have taken an extra half-second, he used muscle, and plenty. Before I could catch up the door banged shut and the lock clicked, and I was standing there with my nose flattened and a big scar across the polished toe of my second-best Bradley shoes.

I took my time descending the three

flights to the ground floor. I was not buoyant. Whenever Wolfe sends me out to bring in something or someone, I like to deliver if possible, but I don't expect to pass miracles. On this one, though, it was beginning to look as if nothing less than a miracle would do, and this was not merely a matter of satisfying a client and collecting a fee. I was the client, and I had roped Wolfe in. It was up to me. But it wasn't like the day before, when I had been on my own and could take a notion to roll down to the Softdown building and crash a meeting; now Wolfe was handling it, and no notion of mine would count without his okay. Added to that, as I made the sidewalk and turned right, deciding not to check out with Halloran across the street, was the difficulty that I had nothing remotely resembling a notion. At Lexington Avenue I got a taxi.

I did not like the way Wolfe took it. When I entered the office alone and announced that as far as I knew no company was expected, then or later, he grunted, settled back in his chair, and requested a verbatim report. Throughout the performance, covering all words and actions with both Sarah Jaffee and Andreas Fomos, he was motionless, his eyes closed and his fingers laced at the summit of his belly, and that was all right; that was perfectly normal. But when I had finished he asked not a single question, only muttering at me, "You'd better type it."

"You mean complete?" I demanded.

"Yes."

"It'll take all afternoon and maybe more."

"I suppose so."

It was true that it was lunchtime, not a moment to expect him to do any digging in, and I skipped it temporarily. But later, after we had been to the dining room and enjoyed a good meal, during which he furnished me with pointed comments on all of the prominent candidates for the Republican nomination for President, I tried again. As he got comfortable with a magazine in his chair behind his desk I remarked, "I could use a program if you can spare the time."

He glared, mildly. "I asked you to type that report."

"Yeah, I heard you. But that was only a stall, and you know it. If you want me to sit here on the back of my lap until you feel like thinking of something to do, just say so. What's the use of wasting a lot of paper and wearing out the typewriter?"

He lowered the magazine. "Archie. You may remember that I once returned a retainer of forty thousand dollars which a client named Zimmermann had paid me, because he wanted to tell me how to handle his case instead of leaving it to me. Well?" He lifted the magazine. He lowered it again. "Please type the report." He lifted it again.

It was absolutely true, and it sounded extremely noble the way he put it, but I was not impressed. He simply hated to work and didn't intend to if he could get out of it. He had given me a chance to get something started, and I had returned empty-handed, and now there was no telling when—or if— he would really get on the job. I sat and looked at him with his damn magazine. It would have been a pleasure to take a gun from the drawer and shoot it out of his hand, and at that angle it would have been quite safe, but I regretfully decided it was inadvisable. Also I decided that nothing I could say or do would budge him right then. I had only two alternatives: take another leave of absence, or obey orders and get busy on the report. I swiveled, pulled the typewriter to me, got paper and twirled it in, and hit the keys.

Three and a half hours later, at six o'clock,

several things had happened. I had typed nine pages. Four journalists had called on the phone, and two in person—not admitted. Fritz had asked me to help him move some furniture in the front room so he could roll up the rug to send to the cleaners, and I had obliged. Wolfe had gone up at four o'clock for his two hours in the plant rooms, and soon afterward there had been a phone call—not from a journalist. I do not gush to strangers on the phone when they ask for an appointment with Wolfe, but when I learned that one's name and the nature of his business it was hard not to. I told him to come at ten minutes to six, and when he arrived, on the dot, I put him in the front room and closed the door that connected with the office.

When Wolfe came down, on schedule, and crossed to his desk, I thought it only fair to give him a chance to show that he had snapped out of it. But no. He sat and rang for beer, and when Fritz brought it he opened a bottle, poured, selected one from the stack of current books on his desk, leaned back, and sighed comfortably. He was going to have a wonderful time until Fritz announced dinner.

"Excuse me, sir," I said gently. "There's

a man in the front room waiting to see you."

His head turned, and a frown appeared. "Who?"

"Well, it's like this. As you explained last night, you had to have some kind of a wedge to start an opening, and this morning I went out to get one and failed. Seeing how disappointed you were, I felt that I must somehow meet the challenge. I have met it. The man in there is a lawyer named Albert M. Irby, with an office on Forty-first Street. I phoned Parker, and he had never heard of Irby but reported back that he is a member of the New York bar in good standing. As for Irby, he says that he is representing Eric Hagh, the former husband of Priscilla Eads, and he would like to talk with you."

"Where the devil did you get him?" It was a blurt of indignation.

"I didn't exactly get him. He came. He phoned for an appointment at four-twenty-one."

"What does he want?"

"To talk with you. Since you don't like a client horning in on a case, I didn't press him for particulars."

Thereupon Wolfe paid me a high compliment. He gazed at me with a severely suspicious eye. Obviously he suspected me of pulling a fast one—of somehow, in less than two hours, digging up Albert M. Irby and his connection with Priscilla Eads, and shanghaiing him. I didn't mind, but I thought it well to be on record.

"No, sir," I said firmly.

He grunted. "You don't know what he wants?"

"No, sir."

He tossed the book aside. "Bring him in."

It was a pleasure to go for that lawyer and usher him in to the red leather chair, but I must admit that physically he was nothing to flaunt. I have never seen a balder man, and his hairless freckled dome had a peculiar attraction. It was covered with tiny drops of sweat, and nothing ever happened to them. He didn't touch them with a handkerchief, they didn't get larger or merge and trickle, and they didn't dwindle. They just stood pat. There was nothing repulsive about them, but after ten minutes or so the suspense was quite a strain.

Sitting, he put his briefcase on the little table at his elbow. "Right off," he said, in a voice that could have used more vinegar and less oil, "I want to put myself in your hands.

I'm not in your class, Mr. Wolfe, and I won't pretend I am. I'll just tell you how it stands, and whatever you say goes."

It was a bad start if he expected any favors. Wolfe compressed his lips. "Go ahead."

"Thank you." He was sitting forward in the big chair. "I appreciate your seeing me, but I am not surprised, because I know of your great services in the cause of justice, and that's what I want, justice for a client. His name is Eric Hagh. I was asked to represent him by an attorney in Venezuela, in Caracas, with whom I had previously had dealings—his name is Juan Blanco. That was—"

"Spell it, please?" I requested, notebook in hand.

He complied and went on to Wolfe, "That was nine days ago, on the sixteenth of this month. Hagh had already sent a communication here to Mr. Perry Helmar, on advice of Blanco, but they had decided that he needed representation here in New York, and Blanco sent me all the particulars of the case, with copies of documents." He tapped the briefcase. "I have them here. If you will just—"

"Later," Wolfe said hastily. "First, what

is wanted?" He looks at documents only when he has to.

"Certainly, certainly." Irby sure was anxious to please. The dewdrops on his freckled cupola might have been glued on. "One of them is a photostat of a letter, a holograph, dated at Cajamarca, Peru, August twelfth, nineteen forty-six, written and signed by Priscilla Eads Hagh and witnessed by Margaret Caselli. That was the maiden name of Margaret Fomos, who was killed Monday night. In the letter Priscilla Hagh gave her husband, Eric Hagh, a half-interest, without reservation, in all property then hers or to become hers at any time in the future."

"Any consideration?" Wolfe demanded.

"Uh—none specified."

"Then it's highly vulnerable."

"That may be. That will have to be adjudicated, but it is unquestionably a powerful weapon, and it was given to my client in good faith and accepted in good faith."

"I'm not a lawyer, Mr. Irby."

"I know you're not, Mr. Wolfe. I came to see you not on a matter of law, but a matter of fact. According to an article in the *Times* this morning, and in other papers, Miss Eads, formerly Mrs. Eric Hagh, was in your house Monday afternoon and

136

evening, and Mr. Perry Helmar, the trustee of her property, was here Monday evening. I would deeply appreciate it, very deeply appreciate it, if you will tell me, in your talks with them was any mention made of this document? Of the letter signed by Priscilla Hagh and witnessed by Margaret Caselli?"

Wolfe stirred in his chair. He rested an elbow on its arm, raised a hand, and ran a fingertip along his lower lip, back and forth. "You'd better tell me more about it," he muttered. "Why did Mr. Hagh wait so long to file a claim?"

"I'm eager to, Mr. Wolfe, I'm eager to. I have it all from Blanco. But of course it would be improper for me to divulge privileged communications, so I won't. I can say this, that Hagh first saw Blanco only a month ago, to show him the document and consult him as to the method of putting in his claim immediately after June thirtieth, his former wife's birthday, when she would come into possession of property worth millions. Blanco got me on the phone, and I checked at this end—chiefly Priscilla's father's will, which of course is on record. With that, and with the details supplied by Hagh, Blanco advised him not to wait for June thirtieth, when the property would pass to Priscilla, but to file his claim immediately with the trustee, Perry Helmar, demanding that half of the property be transferred to Hagh instead of Priscilla, and warning Helmar that he would be held responsible for any default."

Irby raised his shoulders and dropped them. "That may have been good advice for Venezuela. Whether it was for here I don't say. Anyhow Hagh took it, and a communication was sent to Helmar which Blanco wrote and Hagh signed, and a copy of it was sent to Priscilla. A copy came to me too, with photostats of the basic document and a full report of the situation, and instructions from Blanco that I should proceed with an action to restrain Helmar from making the transfer to Priscilla. I know a little law and I know where to find more, but I couldn't find any that would do that trick. Even granting that Hagh's claim was legally valid—"

"I'll take your conclusion, Mr. Irby."

"Very well. I so advised Blanco. He got no reply from Helmar, and none from Priscilla. I finally got to see Helmar—that was last week, Tuesday—and had a long talk with him, but it was completely unsatisfactory. He took no position at all; I couldn't pin him down to a thing. I decided that under the circumstances it would not be unethical for me to see Priscilla Eads. I had already phoned to ask her if Helmar was her personal attorney, and she didn't say yes or no. She refused to see me, but I persuaded her, and called at her apartment Friday afternoon. She admitted that she had signed the document in good faith, but soon afterward had changed her mind and asked Hagh to give it back, and he had refused. She offered to pay a hundred thousand dollars cash in settlement of the claim, and said that if Hagh didn't accept that he would get nothing unless a court ordered it."

"She made you that offer?"

"Yes, and I phoned Blanco in Caracas to report it. June thirtieth was only ten days away, and if Blanco's strategy was sound there was no time to spare. But right there everything died. Blanco called Priscilla's offer contemptible and wouldn't discuss it. Helmar and Priscilla were both away over the weekend, and I couldn't even locate them. Monday morning I started in again, but couldn't get to either one, and I quit trying. Tuesday morning came the news that Priscilla had been murdered. Yesterday."

139

Irby slid back in his chair for the first time. The movement had no effect on the dewdrops. He extended his hands as in appeal. "Think of it!" he pleaded. "The situation!"

Wolfe nodded. "Unsatisfactory."

"Utterly," the lawyer agreed. He repeated it. "Utterly. I saw no point in spending nine dollars on a phone call to Caracas; frankly, it seemed quite possible that there would be no reimbursement for outlay. I did try to get in touch with Helmar, but without success until noon today. I finally got him on the phone, and do you know what he does?" Irby slid forward again. "He impeaches the document! He denies she ever signed it! He implies that my client forged it! And only last Friday she admitted to me unequivocally that she wrote it with her own hand and signed it, and Margaret Caselli witnessed it!"

Irby hit the arm of the chair with his fist. "I phoned Blanco in Caracas!" He hit it again. "I told him to put Eric Hagh on the first plane for New York!" He hit it again. "And bring the original document with him!" He hit it again. "And I decided to see you!"

Abruptly and surprisingly he calmed

down. The fist opened and was only a chubby hand. "Of course," he said, "if millions ever were at stake in this, which is open to question, it is very doubtful if they are now. But even ignoring the Softdown stock, Priscilla's estate is probably substantial, and I do not grant that the stock must be ignored. Even if title to it passes legally to the five persons named in Eads' will, that document is still a powerful moral weapon, especially in view of the time and circumstances of Priscilla's death. And it occurred to me that you can probably speak to the authenticity of the document. She came to consult you that day and spent hours with you. Surely the document was mentioned, and surely she acknowledged that she had signed it. Helmar was here that evening, and he too could have mentioned it and either assumed or acknowledged its validity."

He glanced at me and back at Wolfe. "If Mr. Goodwin was present and can also speak, that will clinch it, and in that case I am prepared to make a concrete offer after discussing it with Blanco on the phone. Such assistance in authentication would be of great value to Mr. Hagh, amounting to five per cent of the total sum received by him in settlement of his claim under the terms of the document."

There were at least two things seriously wrong with it. One, the offer was on a contingent basis, which, while not necessarily disreputable, was against Wolfe's principles. Two, it was an offer to pay us either for telling the truth, which was rather coarse, or for telling a lie, which was downright vulgar.

"Naturally," Dewdrop Irby said, with his voice dripping sugary syrup, "the best form would be affidavits, one from each of you. I'll be glad to draw them, glad and proud, on your information. As for the arrangement for payment to you, I invite your suggestion, with the comment that it is probably inadvisable to put it in writing."

It was a perfect out for Wolfe, and I fully expected to be told to steer the lawyer to the door, but Wolfe is nothing if not contrary. He snapped a question. "Mr. Hagh is coming to New York?"

"Yes."

"When will he arrive?"

"Tomorrow afternoon. Three o'clock."

"I want to see him."

"Certainly. I want you to. I'll bring him

straight here from the airport. Meanwhile, with the affidavits—"

"No." Wolfe was blunt. "There will be no affidavits until I have talked with your principal, and then we'll see. Don't bring him here from the airport; phone me first. I have in mind a step that you won't like but will probably have to assent to. I think there should be a meeting of those concerned in this matter, both sides, with you present, that it should take place tomorrow, and that it should be held in this room. I'll undertake to get Mr. Helmar and his associates here."

Irby was concentrating so hard he was squinting his eyes into narrow slits. "What makes you think I won't like it?"

"The fact that lawyers are convinced that no quarrel involving a substantial sum of money should ever be pursued except by lawyers."

The lawyer would have taken a much worse crack than that without offense. He didn't even feel it. He shook his head earnestly. "I would welcome such a meeting," he declared. "But I would want to have some idea of what I was letting myself in for. If I knew that you and Mr. Goodwin were going to state that both Priscilla Eads and Helmar had either implied or acknowledged the authenticity—"

"No," Wolfe said flatly. "By making me a flagrantly improper offer you have forfeited all right to amenity. You'll have to take it as it comes."

And that was the best Irby could get, though he was so stubborn about it that I finally crossed over to pick up his briefcase and hand it to him, and by then it was dinnertime. When I closed the front door and turned after letting him out, Wolfe was emerging from the office, headed for the dining room.

"Are you satisfied?" he barked at me.

"No, sir," I said politely. "And neither are you."

—9———————————————

The next morning, Thursday, I cashed in on an investment.

I needed some kind of a break. There had been no followup of any kind on the Irby thing. Granted for the sake of argument that after dinner Wednesday evening was no time for it, what was wrong with Thursday morning? I decided for the thou-

144

sandth time that I didn't have the right temperament for working for Nero Wolfe. If I had, I would long ago have quit being exasperated by his matter-of-fact assumption that, barring specific urgencies, there was no point in starting the day's detecting activities until after he came down from the plant rooms at eleven o'clock. And anyway it seemed to me that this was a specific urgency. So when I had got up and shaved and showered and dressed, and gone down and greeted Fritz and had breakfast, and read the morning paper, learning among other things that no one had been charged with the murder of Priscilla Eads or Margaret Fomos, and proceeded to the office and opened the morning mail, and nine o'clock had come and gone with no word from on high, I buzzed the plant rooms on the house phone and got him and inquired, "Do you invite people to the party or do I?"

"Neither, until we're sure of Mr. Hagh." He was gruff, of course.

"He'll land at three."

"Or never."

That was it. One of his deepest convictions was that no vehicle propelled by machinery, from a scooter to an ocean liner, could reasonably be expected ever to reach its destination, and that only a dunce would bank on it. There was nothing I could do about it. After hanging up, I called Pan-Atlantic, and was told that Flight 193 was expected to arrive on schedule. As I got up to put the mail on Wolfe's desk, the phone rang, and I sat down and got it.

"Nero Wolfe's office, Archie Goodwin speaking."

"This is Archie Goodwin?"

"Right."

"This is Sarah Jaffee, Mr. Goodwin."

"So it is, by the voice. Good morning."

"Good morning. I wanted—how are you?"

"I'm fine. And you?"

"I'm fine too. I just had my breakfast and I wanted to phone you. There was no place at the table but mine."

"Good. In the long run that'll save a lot of breakage on dishes."

"It will save more than that." A pause. "You took the coat and hat with you."

"I did, and for God's sake don't tell me you want them back. I disposed of them."

"I'll never want them back." She sounded quite positive. "When I went to the hall, long after you had left, and saw that the coat and hat were gone, I cried like a baby.

When I quit crying I was scared. I was afraid I had been crying because the coat and hat were gone, but then I realized that wasn't it, only I didn't know what it was. Anyhow I quit worrying about why I had cried because I knew one thing for certain—I knew I was glad the coat and hat were gone, and I knew you had done a wonderful thing for me after the way I acted. I guess you understood why I acted like that. I'm a terrible coward, I always have been. I'm such a coward that three times yesterday afternoon when I started to phone you I simply couldn't make my finger turn the dial."

"You could have—"

"No, please! Let me finish or I won't. I slept better than I have for a long time—I don't know when. I had a wonderful sleep! And while I was eating breakfast, there where you were with me yesterday, I realized how it was. I realized that I had to do anything you asked me to do, anything—only, of course not—I mean, anything you *would* ask me—that is, anything I *can* do. So just tell me what it is."

"I told you yesterday."

"I know, but I don't remember it very well."

I explained it carefully, but it didn't seem that she listened carefully, from a couple of questions she asked, so I explained it again. She said she would be at the office at eleven o'clock. I suggested that she bring her own lawyer, and she said she didn't want to tell him about it because he might not approve and she didn't want to argue with him. I didn't insist, since Nathaniel Parker was going to be asked to act on her behalf, and she couldn't possibly do any better.

She warned me, "I don't think I'm still a nut, but I'm still a coward, so I'm pretty brave to do this and I hope you know it."

I told her that I did and fully appreciated it.

That made it a very different kind of morning. First I ascended to the plant rooms and told Wolfe that the thirty cents I had added to my taxi fare by making a detour to the Salvation Army depot had been well invested, and got instructions. Then I returned to the office and obeyed the instructions. The main item was the phone call to Parker, since he had to have full details, including not only names, addresses, events, and intentions, but the purpose and plan of the attack. He was not enthusiastic, which was nothing new; and he made it plain that since he would be Mrs. Jaffee's attorney of record, her interest would be his primary consideration. Knowing as I did that he would give Wolfe his right eye if necessary, I told him that if he got disbarred on account of this operation I could probably get him a job folding paper napkins. I admit it was a feeble crack, but even if it had been a masterpiece he wouldn't have been amused. Lawyers are incapable of taking a joke about getting disbarred because it costs them so much time and money to get barred.

The eleven-o'clock council of war in the office was a big success, with no real argument from anyone. Mrs. Jaffee was ten minutes late, but aside from that I was proud of her, and by the time it was over I was seriously considering calling her Sarah. She was by no means a mere gump, nodding to it just because she didn't know any better. It had to be explained to her in full, exactly what was to be done and why and when and by whom, and for the most part that was left to Parker, since she was his client.

Parker, who is six feet four with nothing to protect his bones from exposure to the weather but tough-looking leathery skin, was so skeptical that at one point I thought he was going to pass, but he finally conceded that the move might be undertaken without undue risk to juridical virtue, to his own reputation, or to his client's life, liberty, and pursuit of happiness. When all details had been settled and money passed—a dollar bill from Sarah to Parker as a token retainer—I got at the phone and dialed a number.

It took persistence. A thin and sour female voice told me that Mr. Perry Helmar was engaged and asked what I wanted. I said that Mr. Nathaniel Parker would tell Mr. Helmar and asked how soon he would be accessible. She said she didn't know. It went on according to pattern, and in order to win I had to drop the name of Mrs. Jaffee. In another minute Helmar was on, and Parker took it at the extension on Wolfe's desk, leaning over on his elbows. I kept my receiver at my ear and got it in my notebook.

After Parker had identified himself as a confrere he dived right in. "I'm preparing to start an action for a client, counselor, and I'm calling you as a matter of professional courtesy. The client is Mrs. Sarah Jaffee. I believe you know her?"

"I've known her all my life. What kind of action?"

Parker was easygoing and anything but pugnacious. "Perhaps I should explain that Mrs. Jaffee was referred to me by Mr. Nero Wolfe. It was on—"

"That crook?" Helmar was outraged. "That damned scoundrel?"

Parker laughed a little, tolerantly. "I won't stipulate that, and I doubt if you can establish it. I was saying that I understand that it was on Mr. Wolfe's advice that Mrs. Jaffee determined on this action. She wants it begun immediately. It is to be directed at Jay L. Brucker, Bernard Quest, Oliver Pitkin, Viola Duday, and Perry Helmar. She wants me to ask a court to enjoin those five people from assuming ownership of any of the capital stock of Softdown, Incorporated, under the provisions of the will of the late Nathan Eads, and from attempting to exercise any of the rights of such ownership."

"What?" Helmar was incredulous. "Will you repeat that?"

Parker did so, and added, "I think it must be admitted, counselor, that this is a new approach and an extremely interesting one. Her idea is that the injunction is to stand until it is determined to the satisfaction of the court whether one or more of those five people has acquired the stock by the commission of a crime—the crime in question, manifestly, being the murder of Priscilla Eads. Frankly, at first I doubted whether such an injunction would be granted, but on consideration I'm not at all sure. It is certainly worth trying, and Mrs. Jaffee, as a stockholder in the corporation, has a legitimate interest at stake. I have told her I'll move in the matter, and at once."

He paused. Nothing for four seconds; then Helmar: "This is an act of malice. Nero Wolfe put Mrs. Jaffee up to this. I intend to speak with Mrs. Jaffee."

"I don't think that will help." Parker was a little chillier. "As Mrs. Jaffee's attorney, I have advised her to discuss the matter with no one—except with Mr. Wolfe, of course, if she sees fit. She is here in Mr. Wolfe's office with me now. As I said, I called you as a matter of professional courtesy, and also because I believe, as I hope you do, that a meeting of minds is always preferable to a meeting of fists or weapons."

"No judge would grant such an injunction."

"That remains to be seen." Parker was close to icy. "I have been discussing it with Mr. Wolfe, who referred Mrs. Jaffee to me. He thinks there should be no delay, and I am leaving now for my office to draft the application, but I told him I thought an effort should be made to protect all interests without going to court. He said he believed any such effort would be fruitless, but he is willing that it be tried, conditionally. The conditions are that it occur this evening, at his office, and that all those involved be present."

"At Wolfe's office?" Helmar was outraged again.

"Yes."

"Never. Never! He's a murderer himself!"

"I think, counselor, you're a little free with words. I know you have been under a strain, but what if you were seriously challenged?"

"All right. But don't think you can get me to agree to come to Wolfe's office. I won't!"

Nevertheless, he did. He didn't come right out and say it, even after he had fully realized that his choice was between that and a summons from a judge to appear and wrangle in public, but he pleaded that he couldn't possibly commit his four associates to such a meeting without consulting them, and he wasn't sure how soon he could get in touch with them. He wanted the afternoon until six o'clock, but Parker said nothing doing. The limit was three-thirty. Parker would proceed to draft the application and have everything in readiness, including a date with a judge, and he would keep the date if by half-past three he had not received word that the Softdown quintet would be at Wolfe's office at nine o'clock that evening.

Parker cradled the phone and straightened up, all seventy-six inches of him. "They'll come," he said confidently but not jubilantly. "Damn you, Wolfe. I have theater tickets."

"Use them," Wolfe told him. "I won't need you."

Parker snorted. "With my client here defenseless? Between them, one of them presumptively a murderer, and you—you a wild beast when you are smelling prey? Ha!" He turned. "Mrs. Jaffee, one of my functions as your attorney is to keep you away, as far as practicable, from dangerous persons and influences, and these two men together represent all the perils and pitfalls of all the catalogues. Will you have lunch with me?"

They left together. That made me proud of her some more from another angle—or should I say curve?—because Nat Parker, a bachelor, was well and widely known for his particular taste in women and did not invite one to lunch absentmindedly; and I was not jealous. I had too good a head start, since there was no more coat and hat in her foyer for him to cart off to the Salvation Army.

Now, of course, Wolfe was committed. He didn't move a finger toward a book or crossword puzzle or any of his other toys. Until lunch time he sat leaning back with his eyes closed, his lips moving now and then, pushing out and pulling in, and I left him to his misery, which I knew was fairly acute. When the going gets really hot and we're closing in, he can get excited as well as the next one, though he refuses to show it, but on this one he was still trying to get set for some kind of a start, and I had to admit he was working at it. Before lunch I phoned Pan-Atlantic and was told that Flight 193 was expected in early, around two-thirty; and I called Irby to tell him that if he could get Eric Hagh to our place by half-past three he should bring him, but otherwise make it six o'clock.

After lunch it was more of the same, with Wolfe being so patient and uncomplaining it was painful, and I would have welcomed a couple of nasty remarks. Shortly before three Parker phoned to say that he had just talked with Helmar and the party was on. The Softdown five would arrive at nine o'clock, and he and Mrs. Jaffee a little earlier. I asked if he was escorting Mrs. Jaffee.

"Certainly," he said virtuously. "She is my client. What's that noise you're making?"

"It's something special," I told him, "and takes a lot of practice. Don't try it offhand. It's a derisive chortle."

I went to the kitchen to discuss the supply of liquid refreshments with Fritz. It was a strict rule that for an evening gathering in that house, whatever the business at hand, assorted drinks must be available, and Fritz and I always collaborated on it unless I was too busy. It always got into an argument, with Fritz insisting that two wines, a red and a white, should be included, and me maintaining that wine was out because it puts Americans to sleep and we wanted them wide awake. We were about ready for the usual compromise—a couple of bottles of white but no red—when the doorbell rang and I went to answer it.

It was Dewdrop Irby with a companion in a white linen suit, somewhat wrinkled and none too clean. I slipped the bolt and opened up and they stepped in.

"Mr. Archie Goodwin," Irby said. "Mr. Eric Hagh."

There had been so much talk of South America that I had been expecting something like a cross between Diego Rivera and Perón, but if this bird had been thoroughly bleached to fit his blond hair and blue eyes I couldn't have told him from a Viking if it hadn't been for his clothes. He was maybe a little older than me, and also, as I would have conceded in spite of his looking fagged and puffy, maybe a little handsomer.

Leaving his luggage, a bag and a suitcase, in the hall, I took them to the office and introduced Hagh to Wolfe. Hagh was inclined to boom when he spoke, but otherwise didn't seem specially objectionable, and I resented it. I was prepared to object to a guy who had married an heiress and got her to sign that document as described, and naturally I felt it was up to him to supply evidence to support my objection. He disappointed me. He did speak with an accent I couldn't place, but I couldn't very well hold that against him with the United Nations only a mile and a half away.

Apparently they were expecting an extended session, from the way they settled in their chairs, but Wolfe made it short and not too sweet. Actually, from our standpoint, those two were now nothing but supers. Irby had been a godsend the day before, when he had come from nowhere to bring us a rake to pull in the Softdown stockholders, but now that Sarah Jaffee had furnished us with a much better one, he and his client were just extras.

Wolfe was moderately polite. "Did you have a tolerable journey, Mr. Hagh?"

"Not too bad," Hagh replied. "A bit bumpy."

Wolfe shuddered. "I congratulate you on your safe arrival." He went to Irby. "There has been a new development. I'm not free to describe it in detail, but it concerns Mr. Helmar and his associates sufficiently for them to have agreed to come here this evening at nine o'clock to discuss the matter. Although—"

"I want to meet them," Hagh said emphatically.

"I know you do. Although they are not coming on your affair, there is no reason why it cannot be broached, since the other matter is closely related. But if you come this evening it must be understood that the procedings are entirely in my hands. You will take part only if and when invited, and you may not be invited at all. Do you wish to be present under those conditions?"

"But," Irby protested, "you said there should be a meeting to discuss my client's claim! I must insist—"

"You are in no position to insist, sir. By making me that silly offer yesterday you forfeited your right to equity. Do you wish to be present this evening?"

"I want only," Hagh said, "what belongs to me—what I can prove belongs to me!"

"I may have worded my offer badly," Irby admitted. "I may have misunderstood the nature of your interest in the matter. But it would be imprudent for us to meet those people here unless we have some assurance that you and Mr. Goodwin are going to testify to the authenticity—"

"Then don't come," Wolfe snapped.

Hagh pulled an envelope from his pocket and waggled it. "I have here the document that my wife signed and Margaret Caselli witnessed. I was present when she wrote it and signed it. It has been in my possession ever since, and there is no honest question that it is genuine. All we want is your help for the truth."

He was absolutely in earnest, probably as much so as he had been on August 12,

1946, when he had finagled Priscilla into signing it. His appeal did not bring tears to my eyes.

Nor to Wolfe's. He said flatly, "There will be no assurance, gentlemen, and no hint of a covenant. I am engaged for the rest of the afternoon. Under the conditions I have proposed, you will be welcome here at nine this evening if you care to come."

That settled it. Hagh wanted him to take a look at the precious document, and Irby was too damn stubborn to give in without a couple more tries, but that was all. They could have saved their breath. I went to the hall with them and was disappointed again when Hagh, who was younger, bigger, and stronger than Irby, insisted on carrying both the bag and the suitcase. I kept looking for little points to score against him, and he kept double-crossing me.

I went to the kitchen and told Fritz there would be nine guests instead of seven.

But as it turned out that was not the final figure. Some four hours later, when I was up in my room changing my shirt and tie in honor of the approaching soiree, the doorbell rang, and a minute later Fritz called up that a man on the stoop who refused to give his name wanted to see me. I finished my grooming and descended and came upon a tableau. Fritz was at the front door, peering at the fastening of the chain bolt. Out on the stoop, visible through the one-way glass, was Andreas Hercules Fomos, glaring angrily at the crack which the bolt and chain were holding the door to, his posture indicating that he was making some kind of muscular effort.

"He's pushing at it," Fritz told me.

I walked to him and called through the crack, "You'll never make it, son. I'm Goodwin. What do you want?"

"I can't see you plain." His voice was even gruffer and deeper than when he had been on the inside talking out. "I want in."

"So did I, and what did I get? What do you want? That's twice, so I have one coming. You asked me three times."

"I could break your neck, Goodwin!"

"Then you'll never get in. I use my neck. What do you want? Now we're even."

A voice came at me from behind. "What is all this uproar?"

Wolfe had emerged from the office and was advancing, which wasn't as impetuous as it might have seemed. It was close to dinnertime, and he would soon have had to mobilize himself anyhow. Fritz trotted off

161

toward the kitchen, where something was probably reaching its climax.

I told Wolfe, "It's Andy Fomos, who ruined a shoe for me yesterday." I told the crack, "In ten seconds we close the door the rest of the way, and don't think we can't."

"What you told me yesterday!" he bellowed.

"What? Do you mean about Priscilla Eads going to make your wife a director of Softdown?"

"Yes! I was thinking about it, and a little while ago I phoned that Mrs. Jaffee. She wouldn't say much, but she told me who you are and said I should see you. If that woman was going to make my wife an important thing like a director there must have been some good reason, and I want you to tell me what it was. She must have owed my wife something big, and I want to know what it was, because if it belongs to me I want it. My wife would have wanted me to have it. And you must know about it, or why did you come to see me?"

I turned to Wolfe. "When you send me out for objects you get 'em, huh? This one completes the order. Do you want it?"

He was standing with his gaze focused through the one-way glass at the visitor.

Fomos was not quite as impressive draped as he had been in shorts, but he was quite a figure. Wolfe grunted. "If he came this evening would he be uncontrollable?"

"Not if I have tools handy, and I will."

"Invite him."

I turned to the crack. "Listen, Junior. Some people are coming at nine o'clock this evening to talk the whole thing over, and we might get around to what's biting you, why your wife was to be made a director, or we might not. You may come if you'll behave yourself. If you don't behave you won't stay."

"I won't wait! I want in now! I want—"

"Oh, can it! You heard me. We're now going to eat dinner, and the thought of you camped on the stoop would annoy us. If you're down on the sidewalk by the time I count ten I'll let you in at nine o'clock. If not, not. One, two, three, four, five, six, seven, eight . . ."

He had made it. Wolfe was headed for the dining room. I went to the kitchen and told Fritz, "One more. There will be ten. Counting Mr. Wolfe and me, an even dozen. Counting you, thirteen."

"Then we will not count me," he said firmly.

─10─

I was mildly peeved at Nathaniel Parker. It had been agreed that he and Mrs. Jaffee would come fifteen or twenty minutes early for a police caucus, and instead of that they were the last to arrive, ten minutes late. Presumably, judging from their manner, they had dined together, and there was no law against that; and also presumably Parker thought a caucus not essential since Wolfe would take charge anyway; but their tardiness made it harder for me. I had no help from Wolfe, since it was his custom, when a gathering was expected, to stay in the kitchen until everyone had assembled.

By the time Parker and Sarah Jaffee showed up the air had got a little thick. The Softdown quintet had not come in a body, but had immediately formed one, collecting over in the corner by the couch and conversing in undertones. When I introduced Eric Hagh and his attorney, Irby, to them, there was no handshaking—for one thing the Softdown group was too surprised. I offered no explanation of Irby's and Hagh's presence, and wasn't asked for one. I did offer drinks, but nobody wanted any. Then Andy Fomos came, and after I had introduced and identified him he mixed himself a long one of white wine and soda and stood apart, sipping his drink and glowering around as if deciding which neck to break first. None but mine, and maybe Hagh's, would have been any problem for him. As for me, I had told Wolfe I would have tools handy, and I had—a snubnosed Farger on my hip and a rubber silencer in my jacket pocket. It didn't seem likely that Wolfe could bring it to a boil at that meeting, but if he did there was no telling who would start what, and I had already had a shoe scuffed.

When Fritz ushered Parker and Sarah Jaffee into the office she stopped just inside the door and looked around. It was the first time I had seen her in artificial light, and she was an attractive sight, with her face a little flushed, in a white summer dress and white slippers, and with a little white bag dangling from her hand. Perry Helmar called her name and started for her, but I intercepted him and got to her and Parker, and claimed attention to pronounce names. Of course none of them had ever seen Parker before, and Irby and Hagh had never seen Sarah Jaffee. Hagh kissed her hand. He had not kissed Viola Duday's hand. Apparently she thought it wasn't a bad idea, from the way she took it, and I admit he was more presentable than he had been that afternoon, now that he was combed and shaved and in a clean white suit and shoes. I maneuvered Perry Helmar into the red leather chair, got the others disposed according to plan, and went to Wolfe's desk and pushed the button, one long and two short.

Wolfe marched in. On account of the crowd, he had to bear right to the wall and follow it to his chair. He stood.

"Archie?" he said.

I identified the four he had never seen. "Miss Viola Duday, formerly assistant to the president of Softdown, Incorporated, and now assistant secretary. Jay L. Brucker, president. Bernard Quest, been with the business sixty-two years, sales manager for thirty-four and vice-president for twenty-nine. Oliver Pitkin, secretary and treasurer of the corporation."

Wolfe inclined his head a full half an inch, for him an elaborate bow, and sat. Before he got satisfactorily adjusted in his chair, which with him took some engineering, Perry Helmar spoke.

"I have prepared a statement," he announced, "which I would like to read." His square jaw was jutting beyond the call of duty. He held a paper in his hand.

"How long is it?" Wolfe asked him.

"Three or four minutes."

"Go ahead."

Helmar adjusted his metal-rimmed glasses, lifted the paper to range, and read:

"Statement by Perry Helmar, June twenty-sixth, nineteen fifty-two. Speaking for myself and of my knowledge, I challenge the propriety of participation by the private detective named Nero Wolfe in any discussion of the affairs of Priscilla Eads, deceased, or of any matters relating to her, including her death. I base this challenge on the fact that the said Nero Wolfe, by his concealment from the undersigned of the presence in his house, on June twenty-third, nineteen fifty-two, of the said Priscilla Eads, and by his gross and premeditated deception of the undersigned, contributed to her peril and thereby became to a considerable degree responsible for her death by violence. The full details of his deception have been supplied to the District Attorney by me in a signed statement, and a copy of that statement is attached hereto in support of this challenge.

I contend that Nero Wolfe is unfit and unworthy to share in any examination of any matters connected with Priscilla Eads.

"Speaking for myself and my four associates, Bernard Quest, Jay L. Brucker, Oliver Pitkin, and Viola Duday, after discussion among us and full agreement, we denounce the said Nero Wolfe for his instigation of an unwarranted attack upon us by Mrs. Sarah Jaffee. We declare that said instigation was prompted by malice, and that the threat of legal action on behalf of Mrs. Jaffee is an unjustified, unprovoked, and reprehensible attempt at coercion. We note that Counselor Nathaniel Parker, who has in the past been associated with Nero Wolfe in many matters, is acting for Mrs. Jaffee, and regard that fact as significant and indicative of the nature of this attempt at coercion, and we demand the right to interview Mrs. Jaffee privately before entering into any discussion with Counselor Parker, and particularly any discussion to which Nero Wolfe is a party."

Helmar lowered the paper. "That is a joint demand," he declared aggressively.

"May I say—" Nat Parker began, but Wolfe showed him a palm.

"If you please, Mr. Helmar. There is no

question of your right to interview Mrs. Jaffee privately, nor is there any question of Mr. Parker's right, and mine, to advise her not to talk with you people except in our presence. The only question is how she feels about it herself. Mrs. Jaffee, do—no. You ask her."

Helmar turned left. He was in the red leather chair, and the other four of the Softdown contingent were on chairs forming an arc running from him in the general direction of my desk. Sarah Jaffee was on the couch. Nearby was Eric Hagh, and beyond him were the two lawyers, Irby and Parker. Andy Fomos was off by himself, over by the bookshelves.

Helmar addressed Mrs. Jaffee. "You wouldn't talk to me on the telephone, Sarah. You have known me all your life. I held you in my arms when you were a baby. Have you ever known me to do anything unfair or dishonest or wicked?"

"Yes," Sarah said. She used more breath than she intended and it caused a sort of explosion, but it was certainly audible.

It rocked Helmar. His eyes popped. "What? Did you say yes?"

"Yes, I did. You did all of those things to Pris. You didn't love her or understand her,

169

and you were bad for her." She lifted her chin a little. "I want to say one thing. I haven't been coerced to do this by Mr. Wolfe or Mr. Parker. I am doing it because I want to, and it was Mr. Archie Goodwin who made me want to. It wouldn't do the slightest good for you to talk with me, Mr. Helmar, or any of the others, so forget it."

"But, Sarah, you don't understand!"

"I think I do. And what if I don't?"

"Skip it, Perry," Viola Duday snapped. "She's hopeless."

"Does anyone else," Wolfe inquired, "have a statement to read?"

Parker put in, "I advise Mr. Helmar not to leave copies of his lying around. It is clearly libelous, as he must know."

Wolfe nodded. "He's upset and not strictly accountable." His eyes moved left to right and back again. "I could reply to Mr. Helmar's indictment of me, but it would take time, and we should get on. First I'll make one thing clear—my status in this business. I have been engaged to investigate the murder of Priscilla Eads, and that is my sole interest."

"By Sarah Jaffee?" Helmar demanded.

"No. My client's identity is not your concern. In my opinion it is entirely proper for

Mrs. Jaffee, as a stockholder in the corporation, to bring the action contemplated, but that will be determined not by my opinion or yours, but by a court. It is certainly proper to submit the matter to a court for decision, and that is what will be done tomorrow morning unless developments here this evening make it unnecessary."

"What developments would make it unnecessary?" That was Oliver Pitkin. Evidently his cold was no better, since he was still sniffling.

"Any of several. For instance, my discovery of the identity of the murderer."

Wolfe's eyes moved deliberately, and other eyes met them. He prolonged it, and no one moved or spoke. "Though I confess," he said, "that I expect no such happy expedition. Another possible development would be for me to conclude, after inquiry, that none of you five people was involved in the murder. Since Mrs. Jaffee's action is grounded on the possibility that one or more of you was involved, and is intended solely to prevent a culprit from profiting from a crime, such a conclusion would make the action needless. The purpose of this meeting is that inquiry by me."

"The purpose of this meeting," Helmar

contradicted, "is an explanation by you and Counselor Parker of this whole outrageous proceeding!"

Wolfe's gaze pinned him. "Do you really mean that?"

"I certainly do!"

"Then get out." He waved a hand. "Out! I've had enough of you!"

They didn't move, except their heads, to exchange looks.

"Before you go," Wolfe said, "here's a piece of information for you. I am told that you are now claiming—specifically you, Mr. Helmar—that the document signed by Priscilla Eads, then Priscilla Hagh, giving her husband a half-interest in her property, is spurious. That is why Mr. Irby is here, and why his client, Mr. Hagh, has come to New York." He focused on Helmar. "If you accuse me of deception, sir, I accuse you of an impudent lie in an attempt to defraud. In this room Monday evening Miss Eads told Mr. Goodwin and me categorically that she had signed that document, and of course you knew—"

"Bravo!" Eric Hagh was out of his chair and moving, pulling an envelope from his pocket. "There is honesty for you, gentle-

172

men!" He waved the envelope. "Here it is! Here it is!"

He may not, judging from his looks, have inherited the South American tendency to exuberance, but he sure had caught it, and there and then someone caught it from him. Andy Fomos bounced up, dashed across, confronted the Softdown team, and boomed, "And before you go you will listen to me! She was going to make my wife a director! And now they are both dead! What can you do, what can you do to make it fair and honest? What you can do is make me a director and pay me what she was going to pay my wife!" He shook a fist, and I got to my feet, but he gave up the fist to point a finger at Viola Duday. "And what were you doing, coming last week to have a secret talk with my wife!" He swung the finger to aim it at Brucker. "And what were you doing, the same thing, coming to talk with her? To ask her to be a director? Huh? Now you can ask me to be a director! There is no—"

"Archie!" Wolfe called sharply. I was already advancing. Others besides Hagh and Fomos were out of their chairs, making a jumble but no tumult.

I got Fomos back to his corner without

serious resistance, and, returning, addressed the Softdown group. "Are you folks leaving or not? If you are, this way out. If not, you must be thirsty, and what will it be?"

"Bourbon and water for me," Viola Duday said promptly.

Wolfe rang for Fritz, and he came in to help, and Eric Hagh offered his services. There was some moving around during the process of serving, and when it was over I noticed that Hagh had homesteaded on the couch with Sarah. Andy Fomos was the only customer for the wine. Wolfe, of course, had beer. I had myself a tall glass of water—not that I don't like something with more authority in off hours, but that hour was far from off. What I wasn't getting in my notebook I was filing in my bean for future reference, and with that bunch I had no faculties to spare.

The idea of a Softdown walkout got no further mention. When all had been refreshed, Helmar stuck his jaw out and began, "On the question of the authenticity of that—"

Wolfe cut him off. "No, sir," he said emphatically. "Your notion of the purpose of this meeting, and Mr. Hagh's notion, and Mr. Fomos's notion, are all different and all

174

wrong. The purpose is an inquiry by me to try to learn whether any or all of you are implicated in the murder of Priscilla Eads. If I decide that you are not, the action by Mrs. Jaffee will be forgone. If I decide that you are or probably are, the action will be pursued."

"This is fantastic," Helmar declared. "We submit to trial on a charge of murder, before you as judge and jury?"

"No, not as you put it. I may not apply sanctions; I have no electric chair in readiness. But if Mrs. Jaffee asks for an injunction, and you dispute it, and the court hears arguments, the degree of probability that one or more of you is implicated in murder will be a major point at issue and will be debated in court. That would be a disagreeable experience for you, and you may be able to prevent it by debating it here, privately, this evening. Do you want to try? If you do, we'd better start. It's ten o'clock."

They looked at one another. "What do you mean by inquiry?" Viola Duday demanded. "Do you mean you question us on anything you please, as the police have? Each of us has spent hours, many hours, with the police."

Wolfe shook his head. "That would take

175

days. I will want to ask some questions—for instance, I shall ask you about the secret talk which Mr. Fomos says you had last week with his wife—but not too many. I propose another method. I suggest an exposition from each of you. You have all been questioned exhaustively by the police, and so should have all pertinent facts and considerations freshly and clearly in mind. Put it this way: I say to you, Miss Duday, there is a suspicion current that you had something to do with the murder of Priscilla Eads, and also of Margaret Fomos, and even that you may have actually committed those crimes with your own hands. What have you to say to remove or discredit that suspicion? You may have half an hour. Well?"

"That's a subtle and dangerous trick, Viola," Helmar warned her.

"How dangerous to the innocent?" Wolfe demanded.

Miss Duday took a sip of her bourbon and water, which was half gone. When she swallowed, a ripple ran down her scrawny neck. There was no sign of lipstick on her. "I think I'll take a chance on the danger," she said in her clear, pleasant voice, "though I doubt if I'll need half an hour. I don't suppose you know, Mr. Wolfe, that in my case the motive was much less weighty than with the others. It is true that I'll get a large block of stock, as they will, but they can outvote me and push me out if they feel like it. Whereas if Priscilla had lived I would soon have been the active head of the corporation, in complete control. That seems pertinent?"

Wolfe nodded. "Mr. Goodwin told me of your comment to him, and Mrs. Jaffee was told by Miss Eads that she intended to make you president. Did you know that Mrs. Fomos was to be a director?"

"Yes. That was because Priscilla wanted all the directors to be women, and we wanted five. She and I and Sarah Jaffee would be three, and a Miss Drescher, a superintendent at the factory, a fourth, and we wanted another, and Margaret had been with Priscilla a long time and was very devoted to her, and we thought it could do no harm and would be a nice gesture."

"That was the only reason?"

"Yes. I will say that I was not enthusiastic about it. Important matters, trade secrets and plans for future operations, are discussed at directors' meetings, and if Margaret attended them naturally she would hear everything. Priscilla trusted her completely, and I had no reason to doubt her, but I wanted to know more about her relations with her husband. Women who are reliably discreet in all other respects will blab anything and everything to their husbands. That was why I went to Margaret's home one evening last week, to meet her husband and talk with both of them and see how they were together. There was nothing secret—"

"No!" Andy was loose again. He came tearing over, declaiming en route. I met him. He decided to come right on through me, and I had either to dive to keep from being trampled or dispose of him, and, choosing the latter, I overestimated his momentum and weight. The result was that my arm twist and hip lift not only repulsed him, they tumbled him and sent him rolling. By the time he got up and started for me I had a chair between us and was displaying the silencer in my hand.

"Hold it, Junior," I told him. "I don't want to bust a knuckle on you, but I think it's time for your nap. Sit down and stay sat, or else." Keeping a corner of an eye on him, I asked Wolfe, "Do you want to let him recite?"

"Not now. We'll see later. Go on, Miss Duday."

She waited for Fomos to return to his chair, then resumed. "My call on Margaret Fomos and my talk with her had no significance whatever other than what I have said. I was talking about motive. Should I deal further with that?"

"Whatever you think might help."

"It will be difficult without giving a false impression, but I'll try. I don't want to give the impression that I think it probable that one of my business associates is a murderer, but facts are facts. Although Priscilla was not fond of me personally, she had great confidence in my intelligence and ability. Also she thought that women should have more positions of power in all fields. And in addition, when she decided some eighteen months ago to take an interest in the affairs of Softdown and learn the ropes, she resented it that the men—and especially the four men present here—treated her with what she regarded as servility but did not conceal—"

Two of them made noises. She halted. Wolfe darted a glance at them. They subsided.

"But did not conceal their doubt of her ability to understand the mysterious process of making and selling towels. If I shared their doubt at all I had brains enough not to show it, and Priscilla appreciated that. More and more she came to me, and only to me, for her lessons and experience. The result was that I had reason to expect great personal advantage from her approaching assumption of ownership and active control. As for what these men had to expect, they can tell you that."

She twisted her lips, considering. "I might add this. In nineteen forty-one when Mr. Eads was alive and I was assistant to the president, my salary was forty thousand dollars. Last year, nineteen fifty-one, with Mr. Helmar in control as trustee, it was eighteen thousand. Priscilla told me that my beginning salary as president would be fifty thousand. Mr. Brucker's is sixty-five."

Wolfe grunted, a little peevishly I thought, possibly at the news that a mere towel merchant was making half as much as him. He asked, "Did these gentlemen know that Miss Eads intended to put you in charge?"

"I'd rather let them answer that. Except— if they say no, may I speak to it?"

"Yes. Go on, Miss Duday."

"Well—as for opportunity, I understand that the theory is that the same person killed both of them, and that Margaret Fomos was

180

killed after half-past ten, and Priscilla was killed before two o'clock. During those three and a half hours I—"

"If you please," Wolfe cut in. "We won't spend time on that."

"No?" Her brows went up.

"No. If one of you has an invulnerable alibi and it has been checked by the police, he can afford to tell me to go to the devil and will surely do so. Moreover, an alibi would convince me of nothing. Consider the crimes. Mrs. Fomos was waylaid on a street at night, dragged or propelled into a vestibule, strangled, and her bag taken. In the bag were keys. Using one of them, the murderer gained access to the apartment of Miss Eads, lay in ambush, and upon her entry struck her and strangled her. Looking at you, Miss Duday, I would think it highly doubtful that you committed those crimes as described, but there is no reason why you shouldn't have contrived them. What would you have to pay? Ten thousand? Twenty? No, I'll leave your alibi or lack of one to the police."

He frowned at her. "As you see, we're severely circumscribed. Motive requires no scrutiny; it blares and brandishes. Means is no problem—a piece of cord two feet long.

181

Opportunity offers no path to a conclusion, since the murders may well have been vicarious, with enough at stake to make them worth planning and paying for. How can I harass you or devise a trap? The best I can do is induce you to talk, and hope for something. How are Mr. Helmar and Mr. Brucker getting along with Miss O'Neil?"

That started a minor commotion. Brucker, who had been letting himself sprawl some, jerked up straight. Pitkin emitted a sound that seemed to be the start of a giggle, but he stopped it. Helmar's jaw fell and then closed and clamped.

Miss Duday kept her composure. "I really don't know," she said. "Of course this has changed the situation—temporarily, at least."

"You told Mr. Goodwin that as soon as Miss Eads was in control Miss O'Neil would lose her job."

"Did I? Well, now she won't."

"You also told Mr. Goodwin that she was playing Mr. Helmar and Mr. Brucker against each other. What was the connection between the fact and the murder of Miss Eads?"

"None that I know of."

"No, that won't do." Wolfe was crisp.

"Mr. Goodwin said he was there to investigate the murder, and you volunteered that information. You are much too intelligent to blatter irrelevancies. What was the connection?"

She smiled a thin tight smile. "Goodness, am I cornered? Do you suppose in some dark crevice of my mind there was the thought that I wouldn't dream of thinking either of those men capable of murdering for profit, but in their blind passion for that creature—there was no telling? And I blurted it out to Mr. Goodwin that day? Am I like that?"

"I couldn't say." Wolfe skipped it. "When and where did you last see Miss Eads?"

"One week ago today. Last Thursday afternoon, at the office."

"What office?"

"The Softdown office at One ninety-two Collins Street."

"What happened, and what was said? Tell me about it."

Viola Duday hesitated. She opened her mouth, closed it again, and hesitated some more. Finally she spoke. "This is a detail," she said, "where we acted like idiots—these four men and I. We had a discussion Tuesday afternoon—it was interrupted by your man, Mr. Goodwin, and we agreed on the account we would give of what had happened on Thursday. We knew that would come up in the investigation of the murder, and we agreed on what to say. It was the only time in my life I have ever been a complete fool. Miss O'Neil was present, because she had been concerned in the events of Thursday. Since she is totally brainless, it didn't take a competent policeman more than ten minutes alone with her to tangle her up. In the end, naturally, they learned exactly what had happened Thursday, so I might as well tell you. Do you want it in full?"

"Full enough. I can always stop you."

"Priscilla came downtown and had lunch with me. She said that she had talked with Sarah Jaffee the day before, and Sarah had refused to be elected a director, that she wouldn't even come to a stockholders' meeting on July first as we had planned. Priscilla and I discussed getting someone else for a fifth director, and other things. After lunch she went back to the office with me. It had got so it was always tense around that place when Priscilla was there, and that day it was worse than usual. I wasn't in the room when the scene between Priscilla and Miss O'Neil started, so I don't know how it began, but I heard the last of it. Priscilla told her to leave the building and not come back, and she refused to go. That had happened once before."

"On the former occasion," Mr. Brucker put in, "Miss Eads had been completely in the wrong."

Viola Duday ignored him. She didn't even spend a glance on him, but kept at Wolfe. "Priscilla was furious. She phoned Helmar at his law office and asked him to come, and when he arrived she told him and Brucker that she had decided to have a new board of directors and put me in as president. They called in Quest and Pitkin, and the four of them spent three hours trying to persuade her that I was incompetent and would ruin the business. I don't think they succeeded. I know that when she left she came to my room and said it would be only eleven more days, and that she was going away for the weekend, and she shook hands. That was the last time I saw her."

"As far as you knew, it was still her intention to make you president?"

"Yes. I'm sure it was."

"Do you know that she came here Monday afternoon and spent some hours in this house?"

"Yes, I know."

"Do you know what she came for?"

"I know nothing definite. I have heard conjectures."

"I won't ask you from whom or what. I am aware, Miss Duday, that in coming here this evening you people were impelled only partly by the threat of a legal action by Mrs. Jaffee. You also hoped to learn what Miss Eads came to see me for and what she said. I'm afraid I'll have to disappoint you. I have given a complete report to the police, or Mr. Goodwin has, and if they don't care to publish it neither do I. But I will ask you, do you know of any reason why, on Monday, Miss Eads should have decided to seek seclusion? Was she being harassed or frightened by anyone?"

"On Monday?"

"Yes."

"I don't know." She bit her lip, regarding him. "Having no knowledge of it, I could only offer a guess."

"Try a guess."

"Well, I know that Perry Helmar had an appointment with her at her apartment for Monday evening. I learned that only yesterday. I know that these men were desperate, and they spent hours Monday at the

Softdown office going through records for years back and compiling memoranda. I thought then that they were probably collecting evidence to prove my incompetence and demonstrate it to Priscilla, and I now think that Helmar made that appointment with her Monday, insisted on it, in order to show her that evidence and convince her that I could not be trusted. My guess is that if she decided to seek seclusion it was because they were pestering her, especially Helmar, and she had had enough of them."

"Why especially Helmar?"

"Because he had more at stake. The others all help to run the business and could expect to continue to get good salaries after Priscilla took over. Helmar has had very little to do with the business operations, and is not an officer of the corporation, but he has been drawing forty thousand a year as counsel. He has actually earned perhaps one-tenth of it, if anything. After June thirtieth I doubt if he would have drawn anything at all, and—"

"That's false, and you know it," Helmar challenged her. "That's utterly unfounded!"

"You'll have your turn," Wolfe told him.

"He can have it now." Miss Duday was

contemptuous. "That's all I have to say—unless you have questions?"

"No. Well, Mr. Helmar? Go ahead."

There was a polite interruption from Eric Hagh. He wanted a refill for his glass, and others were ready too, so there was a short recess. Hagh seemed to have got the impression that we were counting on him to keep Sarah Jaffee company, and I was too busy to resent it, but apparently Nat Parker wasn't.

Wolfe poured beer from his third bottle, swallowed some, and prompted Helmar. "Yes, sir?"

—11—

From his manner and expression it was apparent that it was hard for Perry Helmar to believe that he was in such a fix. For him, a senior member of an old and respected Wall Street law firm, to have to sit conspicuously in that red leather chair and undertake to persuade a private detective named Nero Wolfe that he was not a murderer was insufferable, but he had to suffer it. His oratorical baritone was raspy and supercilious under the strain.

"You say you are not interested," he told Wolfe, "in the factors of means and opportunity. The motive is palpable for all of us, but it is also palpable that Miss Duday is biased by animus. She cannot support her statement that after June thirtieth my income from the corporation would have ceased. I deny that Miss Eads intended to take any action so ill advised and irresponsible."

He took a paper from his pocket and unfolded it. "As you know, when I went to Miss Eads' apartment Monday evening to keep an appointment with her, I found a note she had left for me. The police have the original. This is a copy. It reads:

"Dear Perry: I hope you won't be too mad at me for standing you up. I'm not going to do anything loony. I just want to be sure where I stand. I doubt if you will hear from me before June 30th, but you will then all right. Please, and I mean this, please don't try to find me.
                    Love, Pris."

He folded the paper and returned it to his pocket. "In my opinion, the tone and substance of that communication do not indicate that Miss Eads had decided to repay my many years of safeguarding and advancing her interests in the manner described by Miss Duday. She was neither an ingrate nor a fool. I decline to offer justification of the amount paid to me by the corporation as counsel, but will say only that it was for services rendered. The business is by no means confined solely to making and selling towels, as Miss Duday sneeringly implied. Its varied activities and wide interests require constant and able supervision."

He sent a cold, straight glance at Viola Duday and went back to Wolfe. "However, even if Miss Eads had decided to act as Miss Duday suggests, I would certainly not have been desperate. My income from my law practice, exclusive of the payments from Softdown, is adequate for my needs. And even if I had been desperate I would not have resorted to murder. The idea that a man of my training and temperament would, to gain any conceivable objective, perform so vicious a deed and incur so tremendous a risk is repugnant to every reputable theory of human conduct. That's all."

He clamped his jaw.

"Not quite," Wolfe objected. "You leave too much untouched. If there was no question of desperation, if you had no thought that you were about to be squeezed out, why did you offer me five thousand dollars to find Miss Eads within six days, and double that to produce her, as you put it, alive and well?"

"I told you why. I thought it likely that she had gone, or was going, to Venezuela to see her former husband, and I wanted, if possible, to stop her before she reached him. I had had that letter from him, claiming a half-interest in her property, and she was greatly disturbed over it, and I was afraid she might do something foolish. My using that hackneyed phrase, 'alive and well' had no significance. I told you that the first thing to do would be to check all airplane passengers to Venezuela." He pointed a straight, stern, bony finger. "And you had her here, in this house, and kept it from me. And after I left, you sent her to her death!"

Wolfe, no doubt aware that the finger wasn't loaded, did not counter. He asked, "Then you're conceding that the document Mr. Hagh was waving around is authentic? That his wife signed it?"

"No."

"But she surely knew whether she had

signed it or not. If she hadn't, if it was a fake, why would she go flying off to Venezuela?"

"She was—wild sometimes."

Wolfe shook his head. "You can't have it both ways, Mr. Helmar. Let's get it straight. You had shown Miss Eads the letter from Mr. Hagh and the photostat of the document. What did she say? Did she acknowledge she had signed it, or deny it?"

Helmar took his time replying. Finally he said, "I'll reserve my answer to that."

"I doubt if aging will help it," Wolfe said dryly. "Now that you know that Miss Eads had not gone to Venezuela, and I assure you she had no intention of going, how do you explain her backing out from her appointment with you, her departure, her asking you not to try to find her?"

"I don't have to explain it."

"Do you decline to try?"

"I don't see that it needs more explanation than you already have. She knew that I was coming that evening with documentary proof that Miss Duday was utterly incompetent to direct the affairs of the corporation. I told her so that morning on the phone. I think it likely that she was already aware that she would have to abandon her idea of putting Miss Duday in control, and she didn't want to face me and admit it. Also she knew that Miss Duday would not give her a moment's peace for the week that was left."

"What a monstrous liar you are, Perry," Viola Duday said in her clear, pleasant voice.

He looked at her. That was the first time I had seen him give her a direct and explicit look, and, since she was just off the line from him to me, I had a good view of it. It demolished one detail of his exposition—the claim that a man of his training and temperament couldn't possibly commit a murder. His look at her was perfect for a guy about to put a cord around a neck and pull tight. It was just one swift, ugly flash, and then he returned to Wolfe.

"I should think," he said, "that would explain her leaving and her note to me. Whether it also explains what she said to you I can't say, because I don't know what that was."

"What about Miss O'Neil?"

"I have nothing to say about Miss O'Neil."

"Oh, come. She may be a mere voluptuous irrelevance, but I need to know. What was her manner of play? Was she intimate with both Mr. Brucker and you, or neither? What was she after—diversion, treasure, or a man?"

Helmar's jaw worked. It jutted anyway, and when he gave it muscle it was as outstanding as the beak of a bulldozer. He spoke. "It was stupid to submit to this at all. With the police it's unavoidable, there's no help for it, but with you it's absurd— your ignorant and malicious insinuations about a young woman whom you are not fit to touch. In her innocence and modest merit she is so far above all this depravity—no! I was a fool to come!" He set the jaw for good.

I was gawking at him. It was hard to believe. It is not unheard of for a Wall Street lawyer to find relaxation in the companionship of a well-made female grabber, but when you hear one with his mind still working blathering like that about it, you wonder. Such a man is a menace to healthy and normal dealings between the sexes. After hearing Helmar emit that blah about a specimen like Daphne O'Neil, for weeks I got suspicious whenever I heard myself addressing a young woman in anything more sociable than a defiant snarl.

Wolfe said, "I take it you're through, Mr. Helmar?"

"I am."

Wolfe turned. "Mr. Brucker?"

Brucker was the one I favored. It will sometimes happen, when a group of people are under the blazing light of a murder job, that they all look alike to you, but not often. Usually, sometimes for a reason you can name and sometimes not, you have a favorite, and mine in this case was Jay L. Brucker, the president. I didn't know why, but it could have been his long pale face and long thin nose, which reminded me of a bird I had once worked for during summer vacation in Ohio in my high school days, who had diddled me out of forty cents; or again it could have been the way he had looked at Daphne O'Neil, Tuesday afternoon in the Softdown conference room. There is no law against a man showing his admiration for works of nature, but it had been only a few hours since he had heard of the death of Priscilla Eads, and it wouldn't have hurt him any to wait till sundown to start gloating.

He wasn't gloating now. He was the only one who had had three drinks—a good shot of rye each time, with a splash of water—

and I had noticed that when he conveyed the glass to his lips his hand trembled.

"I would like to tell—" he started. It didn't come through well, and he cleared his throat twice and started over. "I would like to tell you, Mr. Wolfe, that I regard this action by Mrs. Jaffee as completely justified. My opinion was that the stock should be placed in escrow until the matter of Miss Eads' death has been satisfactorily cleared up, but the others objected that sometimes a murder is not solved for months or even years, and sometimes never. I had to admit that their position had some validity, but so has Mrs. Jaffee's, and it should be possible to arrive at a compromise. I do not resent the interest you are taking in the matter. I would welcome and appreciate your assistance in arranging a compromise."

Wolfe shook his head. "You're wasting time, sir. I'm an investigator, not a negotiator. I'm after a murderer. Is it you? I don't know, but you do. I ask you to speak to that."

"I would be glad to"—he cleared his throat again—"if I thought I knew anything that would help you to arrive at the truth. I'm just a plodding, hard-working businessman, Mr. Wolfe; there's nothing brilliant or spectacular about me the way there is about you. I remember a day back in nineteen thirty-two, the worst year for American business in this century. I was an awkward young fellow, had been with Softdown just three years, had started there when I finished college. It was a cold December day, a couple of weeks before Christmas, and I was in a gloomy frame of mind. Word had got around that on account of business conditions further retrenchment had been decided on, and at the end of the year several of us in my section would be dropped."

"If you think this is pertinent," Wolfe muttered.

"I do, yes, sir. On that cold December day Mrs. Eads had come to the office to see Mr. Eads about something and had brought with her Priscilla, their little five-year-old daughter, a lovely little girl. Priscilla remained out on the floor while her mother went into her father's office, walking around looking at people and things, as children will; and I happened to be there, and she came up to me and asked what my name was, and I told her, Jay. Do you know what she said?"

He waited for a reply, and Wolfe, coerced, said, "No."

"She said 'Jay? You don't look like a bluejay!' She was simply irresistible. I had been busy that morning with some tests of a new yarn we were considering, and I had a little of it in my pocket, just a few short strands of bright green, and I took it and tied it loosely around her neck and told her that was a beautiful necklace I was giving her for Christmas, and I took her to a mirror on the wall and held her up so she could look at it."

He had to clear his throat some more. "She was delighted, clapping her hands and making little childish cries of glee, and then her mother came, coming to get her, and with her was the husband and father, Mr. Nathan Eads. And little Priscilla ran to him, to her father, displaying her beautiful green necklace, and do you know what she said to him?"

"No."

"She said, 'Daddy, look what Jay gave me! Oh, Daddy, you can't make Jay go with the others! Daddy, you must keep Jay!' And I was kept! I was the youngest man in my section, and some of my seniors had to go, but I was kept! That, Mr. Wolfe, was the first time I ever saw Priscilla Eads. You can imagine how I felt about her. You can imagine how I have felt about her ever since, through all the years, in spite of all the difficulties and frictions and disagreements. That green necklace, just a scrap of yarn, I put around her little neck! I have of course told this to the police, and they have verified it. You can imagine how I feel now, knowing that I am actually suspected of being capable of killing Priscilla Eads." He extended his hands, and they fluttered. "With these hands! These hands that tied that necklace on her twenty years ago!"

He got up and went to the refreshment table and used the hands, one to hold a glass and the other to pour rye and splash in a little water. Returning to his chair, he gulped half of it down.

"Well, sir?" Wolfe prodded him.

"I have no more to say," he declared.

"You're not serious." Wolfe was flabbergasted.

"Oh, yes, he is." Viola Duday was grimly gratified. "For three years he has written most of the copy for Softdown advertising—but I don't suppose you read advertisements."

"Not ardently." Wolfe eyed Brucker. "Manifestly, sir, either your mental processes are badly constipated or you think mine are. Let's jump twenty years to day before yesterday. Tuesday afternoon you told Mr. Goodwin that you five people—Mr. Helmar was not present, but Miss O'Neil was—had been discussing the murder and had entertained the notion that Miss Eads had been killed by her former husband, Mr. Hagh. You mentioned—"

"Who said that?" Eric Hagh was reacting. He passed between Pitkin and Miss Duday to confront them, and his blue eyes swept the arc as he repeated his challenge. "Who said that?"

Wolfe told him to sit down and was ignored. I got up and headed for him, as Irby, his lawyer, called something to him. I suppose I was more on edge than I realized, with the long session dragging out and obviously getting nowhere, and it must have shown on my face that I was ready to plug someone and why not Eric Hagh, for Wolfe called my name sharply.

"Archie!"

It brought me to. I stopped short of Hagh and told him, "Back up. You were to take part only if and when invited."

"I've been accused of murder!"

"Why not? So has everyone else. If you don't like it here, go back where you came from. Sit down and listen and start cooking up a defense."

Irby was there with a hand on his arm, and the big handsome chiseling ex-husband let himself be urged back to his seat in the rear.

Wolfe resumed to Brucker: "Regarding Mr. Hagh, you said that he wouldn't even have had to come to New York, that he could have hired someone to kill his former wife. What was the significance of your suggestion that the deed had been done by a hired assassin?"

"I don't know." Brucker was frowning. "Was it significant?"

"I think it may have been. In any case, I am impressed by your enterprise in hustling off to Venezuela for a candidate when there was no lack of eligibles near at hand. But the question arises, what was in it for Mr. Hagh? Why did he want her dead?"

"I don't know."

"Someone would have to know. Miss Duday offered the singular suggestion, to Mr. Goodwin, that Miss Eads had denied she had signed the document, or Mr. Hagh thought she was going to, and so he had to destroy her. That is doubly puerile. First, she had acknowledged that she had signed the document. Second, she had offered, through Mr. Irby, to pay one hundred thousand dollars in settlement of the claim—just last week. Whereupon Mr. Hagh, in a fit of pique, dashes to the airport for a plane to New York, flies here and kills her, after first killing her maid to get a key, and flies back again. Does that sound credible?"

"No."

"Then arrange it so it does. Why did Mr. Hagh kill his former wife?"

"I can't tell you."

"That's a pity, since the simplest way for you people to make me doubt your guilt would be to offer an acceptable substitute. Have you one?"

"No."

"Have you anything else to offer?"

"No."

"Do you wish to make any comment on what has been said about Miss O'Neil?"

"I do not."

Wolfe's gaze went left. "Mr. Quest?"

—12——

During the fifty-some hours that had passed since my call at the Softdown building on

Collins Street, I had had plenty of spare moments for research, and one of the items I had collected was Bernard Quest's age. He was eighty-one. Nevertheless, it was not necessary to assume, as Wolfe had in the case of Viola Duday, that if he had killed Priscilla Eads he had probably done so by contrivance and not by perpetration. In spite of his pure white hair and wrinkled old skin, I would have bet, from the way he looked and moved and held his shoulders and head, that he could still have chinned himself up to five or six times.

He told Wolfe, in a low but firm and strong voice, "In a long life I have had to swallow only two really bitter pills. This affair is one of them. I don't mean the murder, the violent death of Priscilla Eads, though that was shocking and regrettable. I mean that it is thought possible that I, Bernard Quest, was involved in it. Not only by you, I don't care about you, but by the official and responsible investigators of crime."

His eyes went left, to Pitkin and Miss Duday, and right, to Brucker and Helmar, and back to Wolfe. "These others are infants compared to me. I have been with this business sixty-two years. I have been sales manager for thirty-four years and vice-president for twenty-nine. More than four billion dollars' worth of our products have been sold by me and/or under my direction. In nineteen twenty-three, when I was made vice-president by Nathan Eads, he promised me that someday I would be given a substantial block of stock in the corporation. In the years that followed that promise was repeated several times, but it was never kept. In nineteen thirty-eight Nathan Eads told me that he had made provision in his will for redemption of the promise. I protested, and by then I was resentful enough to back up my protest with action, but it was too late. I was nearly seventy years old, and rival firms which had formerly offered me unlimited inducements would no longer do so. By then I knew, of course, that I could place no reliance at all on the word of Nathan Eads, but I had waited too long to make my demands effective by the only method that would have moved him.

"Four years later, in nineteen forty-two, he died. When the will was read I found that once more he had broken his word to me. I said I have swallowed two really bitter pills; that was the first one. It may be asked, what did it matter? I was over seventy. My children were grown and out in the world, happy and on the way to success. My wife was dead. I had an ample income, more than I needed. What good would three million dollars' worth of corporation stock have done me? None. None at all. Probably more harm than good to me and mine. But I decided to kill a girl, Priscilla Eads, then fifteen years old, in order to get at least a portion of it."

"Bernie!" Miss Duday gasped.

"Yes, Vi." He looked at her, nodded, and returned to Wolfe. "I have not told this to the police, not because I thought it important to withhold it, but because those who have questioned me have not been a stimulating audience. Sitting here an hour ago, I realized that it would be—a pleasure? No, not a pleasure, but an excellent opportunity to lighten the load. After eighty, that is a major objective, to lighten the load."

Suddenly he smiled, but it was not at or with any of us; he was smiling to himself. "My sense of justice, of fairness, was outraged. I knew that Nathan Eads, who had inherited the business, had contributed very little to its phenomenal growth during the quarter-century he had been the nominal head. That growth was mainly the work of two men, one named Arthur Gilliam, a production genius, and me. Eads had to give Gilliam ten per cent of the corporation's stock in order to keep him, and that stock is now owned by Gilliam's daughter, Mrs. Sarah Jaffee. Because I wasn't as tough as Gilliam, I got nothing. And this final treachery of Nathan Eads in the provisions of his will was too much for me. I didn't decide to kill Priscilla for the sake of gain; that would have been a rational decision, and it wasn't rational at all; I was simply unbalanced. I suppose I was actually insane."

He waved that aside. "I decided," he said, "to strangle her."

There was a stir in the audience. He ignored it. "I knew that many criminals are traced by laboratory analysis of an object or objects, and I took elaborate precautions against that danger. Needing a piece of cord, I spent many hours reflecting on the safest method of getting one. My home was in Scarsdale, with a yard and a garage, and of course there were several kinds of cord around the place that would have served, but this must be absolutely untraceable. I solved the problem ingeniously, I think. I took the Broadway subway to the end of the line and went for a walk. Within half an hour I had spied two or three that would have been all right, but I was particular. The one I selected was at the edge of a vacant lot not far from the sidewalk—a piece of clothesline about three feet long. There was no passer-by within a hundred paces, but I was careful. I stooped to tie a shoe-lace, and when I straightened up the cord was coiled tightly in my hand."

Viola Duday demanded, "Are you inventing this, Bernie?"

"No, Vi, this happened. I stuffed the cord in my pocket immediately and left it there until I was at home alone in my bedroom with the door locked. Then I examined it and was pleased to find that though it was very dirty and worn some it was quite sound. I went to the bathroom and washed it well in soapy water and rinsed it, but was then confronted with a problem. Where could I leave it to dry? Of course not where there was the slightest risk of its being seen by one of my two servants or by one of my guests who were coming to dinner, and I didn't want to lock it in a drawer, wet. I didn't like the idea of locking it in a drawer at all. So, after taking a shower, I tied the cord around my waist before dressing for dinner. I was quite uncomfortable with that cord around me next to my skin, but I wouldn't have been comfortable if I had put it anywhere else.

"Later, after my guests had gone, when I was undressing for bed, I was reflecting on another problem, not for the first time. Would I have to make her manageable by hitting her with something before using the cord? I thought it greatly preferable to use only the one weapon, the cord, if it could be done that way. Removing it from my waist, I tried encircling various objects with it—the arm of the chair, a book, a pillow—and pulling it tight, but that told me nothing. I had to know how much tension was needed to choke off air and sound and make her helpless quickly. So I put the cord around my neck, got a good hold, and started to pull."

All eyes were fixed on him as he lifted his fists to touch knuckles beneath his chin, and slowly to begin parting them.

"My God," someone said.

Quest nodded. "Yes, but it's anticlimax. No one came to me just in time. I merely came to myself, after collapsing on the floor and lying there naked some minutes—I don't know how many. Nor do I know whether my collapse was only psychological or physical, or was physically induced by my tightening the cord. I do know that that was the one time in my life when the notion of suicide has flashed into my mind—not when I put the cord around my neck and pulled on it, I was conscious of no such notion then—but after I came to. For a moment my mind was quite empty. I sat on the floor staring at the cord in my hand— and suddenly it all rushed in on me as if a dam had burst. I had been seriously and deliberately planning murder, and there was the cord to prove it! Or had it been just a nightmare? I clambered to my feet and went to a mirror to look, and there was a livid ring around my neck. If at that moment there had been an easy way at hand—say, a loaded gun—I think I would have killed myself. But there wasn't, and I didn't. Later on, toward morning, I believe I even slept.

"Well." Quest gestured. "That was the end of that. For ten years that cord, neatly coiled, has been on a tray on my dresser, where I see it morning and night. I have often been asked what it is and why it is there, but I have never told until now. As I—"

"Is it still there?" Wolfe asked.

Quest was startled. "Of course!"

"Has it been there continuously?"

Quest was more startled. His mouth dropped open, and his jaw hung, making him look ten years older. When he spoke his voice was different. "I don't know." He sounded half dazed. "I haven't been home since Monday morning. I've been staying with my son in town—I want to phone." He was on his feet. "I want to phone!"

I told him, "Here," and pulled the instrument across and got up, and he came and took my chair and dialed a number. After a long wait he spoke.

"Della? . . . No, no, this is Mr. Quest. I'm sorry to get you out of bed. . . . No, no, I'm quite all right. I just want you to do something for me. You know that piece of old clothesline on the tray on my dresser? I want you to go and see if it's there just as it was, just the way it was. I'll hold the line. Go and see and come and tell me. . . . No, don't move it, just see if it's there."

He propped his forehead on his free hand and waited. All eyes were not on him, because there were glances at Wolfe, who had reached for his own instrument and was listening in. Two full minutes passed before Quest's head lifted and he spoke.

"Yes, Della. . . . It is? You're sure? . . . No, I just wanted to know. . . . No, no, I'm all right, everything's quite all right. . . . Good night."

He put the receiver on the cradle, accurately and firmly, and turned. "I could have used it, Mr. Wolfe, that's true, but I couldn't possibly have put it back, because I haven't been there." He stood up, got a change purse from a pocket, took out two dimes and a nickel, and put them on my desk. "It's a quarter call with tax. Thank you." He returned to his chair and sat. "I think it will be better if I restrict myself to answering questions."

Wolfe grunted. "You've anticipated them, sir. That was well conceived and superbly executed, flummery or not. You have nothing to add?"

"No."

"So you also know when to stop." Wolfe went right. "And you, Mr. Pitkin? Were you too blessed with a catharsis many years ago?"

Oliver Pitkin sniffed for the hundredth time. A rye and ginger ale had been provided for him some two hours back, and he was still working at it. I had been wrong about him Tuesday when I figured that he had always been fifty years old and always would be. He had already put on at least five years, and he had shrunk. Instead of tagging him a neat little squirt I would now call him a magnified beetle. Apparently he had heard somewhere that it is impressive, when you are conversing, to keep your head tilted forward with your chin on your chest, and to look up from under your brows, like a prizefighter in a crouch—and maybe it can be, but not when he did it.

"I'm not sure," he said cautiously, "that I know what a catharsis is. Will you define it?"

"I'd rather withdraw it. Let's revert to my question to Miss Duday: what have you to say to remove or discredit the suspicion that you are a murderer?"

"That's not the way to do it." He sniffed. "That's un-American. First show me the evidence back of the suspicion, if there is any, and then I will answer it. That's the American way."

"I have no evidence."

"Then you have no suspicion."

Wolfe regarded him. "Either, sir, you're an ass or you're masquerading as one. When there is evidence that you have murdered, there will be not a suspicion but a conviction. If I had evidence that one or more of you is guilty I wouldn't sit here half the night, inviting you to jabber; I would phone the police to come and get you. Have you anything to say?"

"Not like that, no. Ask me a question."

"Do you think you are capable of committing a murder—not killing in defense or an explosion of passion, but deliberate murder?"

Pitkin studied him from under his brows. He wasn't going to be caught off guard. "No," he said.

"Why not? Many people can and do. Why couldn't you?"

That took more study. Finally: "Because of the way I look at things."

"How do you look at things?"

"From the standpoint of profit and loss. I'm a bookkeeper, and, the way I see it, there's nothing to life but bookkeeping. That's why Mr. Eads kept promoting me until he made me secretary and treasurer of the corporation—he knew how I looked at things. One rule is this: that if the risk of a transaction is very great it should not be considered at all, no matter what profit it offers if it is successful. That's one of the basic rules that should never be broken.

213

You apply that rule to the idea of committing a murder, and what do you get? There's too much risk, so you don't do it. The idea is no good. It's all a matter of debit and credit, and with murder you start out with too big a debit. Every proposition on earth can be figured on a basis of profit and loss, and there's no other practical way to figure anything."

He sniffed. "When I say profit I mean earned profit, but not in the legal sense. I mean earned *de facto*, not *de jure*. Take the income I will get for the rest of my life from my ownership of stock in Softdown, Incorporated. That is called unearned income, but actually I have earned it by the years of devoted service I have rendered to the company. I have earned it because I deserve it. But as a contrast, take the profit—the income—that Sarah Jaffee has been getting from her ownership of stock since the death of her father."

He twisted around in his chair. "Mrs. Jaffee, I'd like to ask you, what have you ever done for the corporation? Tell me one single thing, small or large. Your average income in Softdown dividends for the past five years has been more than forty thousand dollars. Have you earned one cent of it?"

Sarah was staring at him. "My father did the earning," she said.

"But you, personally?"

"No, of course not. I've never earned anything."

Pitkin left her. "And take you, Mr. Hagh. What your claim amounts to in reality—you are demanding a share of the Softdown profits. Legally you may get something, I don't know, but you certainly haven't earned anything, and nobody related to you or connected with you has earned anything. Isn't that correct?"

Hagh's expression was tolerant. "It is perfectly correct, sir. I can feel no regret or embarrassment at being put in the class with the charming Mrs. Jaffee." He smiled irresistibly at Sarah, who was next to him.

Pitkin untwisted to his normal position, focusing on Wolfe from under his brows. He sniffed. "You see what I mean when I say that life is nothing but bookkeeping?"

Wolfe nodded. "It's not too recondite for me. How about Miss Eads? Wasn't her position essentially the same as Mrs. Jaffee's? Wasn't she also a parasite? Or had the interest she had recently shown in the business made her an earner?"

"No. That was no service to the corporation. It was an interference."

"Then she had earned nothing?"

"That's right."

"And deserved nothing?"

"That's right."

"But in a week she would have taken title to ninety per cent of the company's stock, leaving you earners with nothing but your salaries. Wasn't that deplorable?"

"Yes. We all thought so."

"You, perhaps, with uncommon warmth because you are fiercely anti-feminist and hate to see a woman own or run anything?"

Pitkin sniffed. "That is not true."

"So Miss Duday told Mr. Goodwin."

"Miss Duday is spiteful and untrustworthy. About women, I merely feel that they too should be subject to the rules of bookkeeping and be permitted to take only what they earn, and on account of their defects of ability and character they are incapable of earning much more than a bare subsistence. The exceptions are very rare."

Wolfe pushed his tray back, placed his palms on the chair arms, and moved his head slowly from left to right, from Helmar to Duday, and back again, taking them in.

"I think I've had enough of you," he said, not offensively. "I'm not at all sure the evening has been well spent—whether, as Mr. Pitkin would put it, it shows a profit or loss, for you or for me." He levered himself out of his chair and upright. "Mr. Parker, will you come with me? I'd like to consult you briefly before deciding where I'm at."

Taking the wall detour as before, he headed for the door, where Parker joined him, and they left together. I got up and canvassed for refills and got some takers, most of them leaving their seats. Viola Duday herded Sarah Jaffee to a far corner for a tête-à-tête. Andy Fomos crossed to them and joined in, uninvited; but in spite of their defects of ability and character they showed no signs of being in distress, so I didn't intrude. When everyone had been attended to at the bar, I propped myself on the edge of Wolfe's desk and closed my eyes and listened to the little hum they were making. I agreed with Wolfe—I had had enough for now, chiefly because I had caught no glimmer. Had he? I squeezed my eyes tight, concentrating, and the hum of the crowd kept me from hearing the door opening, but the hum stopped suddenly, and I raised my lids. They had returned. Parker crossed to Sarah. Wolfe came to his chair behind his desk but did not sit. He faced them.

"Miss Duday and gentlemen. I am not prepared to say yes or no. It's past midnight, and I must digest what I have heard and seen. I make only this commitment: Mr. Parker will take no step on behalf of Mrs. Jaffee until he has heard from me sometime tomorrow, and he will notify you in advance through Mr. Helmar."

Of course it wasn't that easy. Helmar objected, and Brucker, but the loudest and stubbornest protests came from Irby, Eric Hagh's lawyer, and Andy Fomos. Irby wanted the authenticity of his client's document explicitly acknowledged by everyone. Fomos wanted to know when he would be made a director and how much he would be paid. While that minor tumult was proceeding, Bernard Quest went quietly to Sarah Jaffee and spoke to her persistently, but I saw her shake her head several times, so apparently he wasn't doing so well.

First to give up and go was Fomos. He suddenly threw up his arms and dashed for the hall, and I had to step on it to get there in time to see him disappearing onto the stoop. Next was Viola Duday, with no escort, and then Jay Brucker and Oliver Pitkin together. Bernard Quest left alone, and Perry Helmar. The only one who thought it appropriate to offer me a hand to shake when I let him out was Eric Hagh, who left with his lawyer, Irby. Last to go were Sarah Jaffee and Nathaniel Parker. I felt magnanimous as I closed the door after them and put the bolt on. What the hell, let him take her home. I was still way ahead, with my coat-and-hat-disposal service.

As I started for the office, here came Wolfe, headed for his elevator.

"Which one?" I asked.

He halted, glaring. "Which one what?"

"Excuse me. I meant it only as a pleasantry. If you're as stumped as you look, God help your client."

He eyed me. "Archie. Do you know who killed Miss Eads and Mrs. Fomos?"

"No, sir."

"Do you think you know?"

"No, sir."

"I do—or I did—but there's a contradiction. What about Mrs. Jaffee? Is she a snake or a cheat?"

"No. Nice odds, say ten to one."

"Then I need to ask her something, after consideration. Will you please have her here in the morning at eleven?"

I told him yes, and he proceeded to his elevator. My bed would have to wait a little, until I had helped Fritz put the office in order, especially ashtrays and the remains of the liquid refreshments. He was already in there, and I went to join him.

—13——————————

It was a hot night, and I had only a sheet over me, and it only up to my waist, so when the jangle of the phone roused me enough to realize what it was, my arm was free to reach and bring it to my ear. Awakened by it at night, I do not tell it, "Nero Wolfe's residence, Archie Goodwin speaking." For one thing, I am too indignant at the interruption, and for another, I am only one-fifth awake and not absolutely sure who or where I am.

"Yeah?" I said bitterly.

"Is this Nero Wolfe's house?"

The voice got me one-half awake. "Yes. Archie Goodwin."

"This is Sarah Jaffee. I'm awfully sorry, Mr. Goodwin, did I wake you up?"

"Not quite. Go ahead and finish it."

"I guess I should have waited until morning, but I thought you might have found them and wondered whose they were. Did you find any keys?"

"No. Why, did you lose some?"

"Yes, two on a ring, to the door downstairs and my apartment. They were in my bag."

"Where are you now?"

"I'm home in the apartment. I might—"

"How did you get in?"

"The elevator man. The night man has a key. I might have lost them in the Flamingo Club or the taxi, but I thought I ought to phone you in case you found them. I'm so sorry I bothered you. Good night."

"Wait a minute." I was sitting on the edge of the bed now, with the light on. The clock said ten minutes to two. I was fully awake. I didn't want to scare her stiff, but the situation did not seem ideal. "Don't ring off," I told her. "Is Olga there?"

"No, she doesn't sleep here."

"You went to the Flamingo Club with Parker?"

"Yes, we stopped for a drink and a dance."

"When did you miss the keys?"

"While I was coming up in the elevator. I went to get them from my bag, and they weren't there."

"Why not downstairs on the sidewalk?"

"I didn't look for them there. The night man was there with the door open."

"And Parker didn't go up with you."

"No."

"Okay. Don't ring off. Keep that phone at your ear and mouth."

"Why—what—"

"Nothing. A million to one it's nothing—you lost some keys, that's all. But after what happened Monday night I'm nervous about keys, and you might as well humor me. After the night man let you into the apartment, how long were you there before you phoned me?"

"I called you right away. I wanted to get you before you were asleep. What do you mean, you're nervous about keys? You don't—"

"I mean I like you to some extent in spite of the bum coffee Olga makes, and I'm coming up there right away just to make sure. Where's the phone you're talking from?"

"In the living room."

"That's at the other end from the foyer?"

"Yes. Did you say you're coming up here?"

"Right. Will you take instructions from me?"

"I will if—yes. Of course." Her voice was not steady.

"Then listen. This is almost certainly a false alarm, but listen anyway. Don't ring off. When I say, 'Go ahead,' you say this to me, quote 'I don't think so, but if you'll hold the line I'll go to the foyer and see if it's there.' Unquote. Do you want me to repeat that?"

"No, you don't need to."

"Sure you've got it all right?"

"Yes."

"Good. As soon as you say that, put the phone down—just put it down, don't ring off—and walk to the foyer, go straight to the outside door, open it and pass through and pull it shut with a bang. Go to the elevator and push the button, and keep your finger pushing the button until the elevator comes. Go downstairs with the elevator man and wait there till I come. Did you get all that?"

"Yes."

"Will you do it just that way?"

"Yes, I—I will."

"That's the girl. Don't forget to bang the door, because I'm going to keep the phone to my ear until I hear the door bang, and then I'll start. After I get there you can have a good laugh at me for being so nervous, and then we'll decide what to do next. For one thing, I'm a better dancer than Nat Parker, and it's only two o'clock. Are you listening?"

"Yes."

"I'm repeating it. When I say, 'Go ahead,' you say, 'I don't think so, but if you'll hold the line I'll go to the foyer and see if it's there.' As soon as you say that, put the phone down, go to the foyer, open the outside door, go out, bang the door shut, ring for the elevator, and keep your finger on the button until it comes. Go downstairs and stick with the night man until I arrive. Wherever he goes, you go. Will you follow instructions?"

"Yes."

"Are you all set?"

"Yes."

"Go ahead."

"I don't think so, but will you hold the line? Uh-hold the line, and I'll go and see if it's in the foyer."

Good enough, I thought, with no rehearsal. There was a little clatter as she put the phone down. I could hear no footsteps, but the living room had rugs. Figuring that fifteen to twenty seconds ought to do it, and that thirty was the maximum if there were no snags, I started counting as I heard the phone drop. I can count and never be out more than three seconds in five minutes. As I counted I remembered that I had told Wolfe, when he gave Priscilla Eads eleven hours to hide, that it was like run sheep run, but this was more like prisoner's base. The phone in the living room was one base, and the elevator outside was the other, and it was up to Sarah Jaffee to make the run without being tagged. It had been a lot of years since I had played prisoner's base.

That had darted through my mind by the time I had counted ten. From then on the strain of listening kept it empty. If she gave it a healthy bang I would unquestionably hear it. I got to fifteen, to twenty—no bang. Thirty. I had the phone pressed to my ear. Forty, fifty, sixty—a full minute. It couldn't

225

possibly have taken her that long, but I held onto the damn thing, counting automatically—ninety-four, ninety-five, ninety-six . . .

I hung up, with my brain humming, but one thing was a cinch—I needed clothes. As I got them on, I considered. If I spent time calling the Nineteenth Precinct, which was nearest to her, I might or might not get a lieutenant who preferred acting or arguing, especially since my one fact was that a woman's keys were missing. There were several possible explanations for my not hearing the door bang, including the chance that she had failed to bang it. Various alternatives to calling the precinct offered themselves, but by the time I was dressed, and that wasn't long, they had all been discarded.

I ran downstairs to the office, got a gun and dropped it in my pocket, fixed the phone to ring on Fritz's and Wolfe's extensions, returned to the hall and descended to the semibasement, entered Fritz's room, and gave him a shake. He let out a yelp.

"Out on a errand," I told him. "I'll be back when you see me."

He warned me to be careful, as he usually does when I leave the house on business, but I didn't hear it all because I was on my way, out through the area door and up four steps to the sidewalk. I headed east at a trot. At that time of night taxis on Tenth Avenue are none too frequent, and I made for Thirty-fourth Street and finally got one. Tenth Avenue was no good, with its staggered lights, so I had him go east to Park, and up Park. He did all right, as he should have with the finif I gave him in his pocket, and with that avenue as nearly open as it ever gets. When we turned into Eightieth Street, with the tires squeaking, it was 2:23, just twenty-six minutes since I heard her put the phone down. As we rolled to the curb in front of the address, I had the door open and was on the sidewalk before the car stopped. I had told the driver to wait, and had shown him my license to clear the way for some hasty request if I had to make one.

There wasn't a soul in sight. I went to the entrance door and tried it; it was locked. As I rattled it, peering in, a man in uniform appeared from around a corner, approached, touched the glass with his forehead, and looked out at me.

"What do you want?" he called.

"I want in!"

"For what?"

"To see Mrs. Jaffee. I'm expected."

"At this time of the night? Nuts. What's your name?"

It was hopeless. This one had never seen me; he had not been on duty when I came Wednesday morning. He was obviously an underbrained dope. It would take minutes to explain, and he wouldn't believe me. If I persuaded him to ring her on the house phone and there was no answer, he would probably say she was asleep. I took the gun from my pocket, let him see what it was, knocked a hole in the glass with it, reached through and opened the door, and entered. As I did so I heard the engine of the taxi roaring, and a glance over my shoulder showed it starting off. That boy had fast reflexes.

I was pointing the gun at the dope, and he was standing with his arms straight up as far as he could reach. There wasn't a chance in a million that he was accoutered, but I gave him a few quick pats to make sure. "Have you seen Mrs. Jaffee in the last half-hour? Or heard her? Talk fast. Have you?"

"No! She came—"

"Into the elevator. Step on it! Sixth floor."

He obeyed. We started up. "You're crazy," he said. "That hackie will have a cop here in no time."

I saved my breath. The cage stopped. "On out," I told him, "and to Six B." He hooked the door open and preceded me along the hall. At the door of 6B he put his thumb to the button.

"I'll do that," I said. "You get out your keys and open the door."

"But I'm not supposed—"

That dope never knew how close he was to getting slammed down with a hunk of metal. I knew damned well I was too late, and it would have helped a little to clop eight or nine people, beginning with him. But as I gave the gun a jerk he went for his keys. For the record, I pressed a finger against the bell button and kept it there while he was unlocking the door. When he had it open I pushed him through ahead of me, but only two steps in he stopped, and I quit pushing.

She was lying off to the right, about half-way to the entrance to the living room, her body in a twisted position, one leg straight out and one bent. Her face was in full view from where we stood, and there was no question about being too late, as was natural in a case of throttling. She was not recognizable.

The dope made a movement, and I grabbed his arm and whirled him around.

"Christ Almighty," he said, and it looked as if he were about to blubber.

"Take the elevator down," I told him, "and stay there. The cops will want it."

I shoved him out and closed the door and turned. There was no time for a job, but a glance was enough. She had followed instructions all right, but had never reached the outside door. Three paces from where she lay a closet door was standing open. He had been ambushed there, and, as she passed, had swung the door open and hit her with a bronze tiger, a bookend. It was there on the floor. He had then finished up with a doubled cord from a venetian blind, also there on the floor. Everything was right there.

I went to her and squatted and tried to push the tongue back in, but it was too swollen. That and the eyes were plenty, but I picked a few fibers from the rug and put them over her nostrils and counted ten slowly. No. I got up and went to the living room and crossed to the table where the phone was. Yes, she had followed instructions; she had not rung off.

I picked up the receiver and cradled it,

waited ten seconds, picked it up again, got the dial tone, and dialed a number. After only three rounds Wolfe's voice came. He was a sound sleeper, but it didn't take a sledgehammer to wake him.

"Hello?" He was as indignant as I had been.

"Archie. Get this, because we may be interrupted. Sarah Jaffee phoned me. Her keys were missing from her bag, and the elevator man had let her in. I said I would go up to her and told her what to do meanwhile. I came, and I'm phoning from her apartment. She did what I told her to, but she's here on the floor dead. Hit on the head and then strangled. The next time she's in danger she should phone someone else. I don't know when I'll be home."

"Archie."

"Yes, sir."

"I said it is vainglorious to reproach yourself for lack of omniscience. That is also true of omnipotence. Report in as you can."

"Right. Happy dreams."

I pressed the knob down and held it for a moment, let it up, and dialed WA 9-8241. There I got a break, and I never needed one more—Sergeant Purley Stebbins was on duty. I will not claim that Purley loves me,

231

but at least he will listen sometimes. I got him.

"Yeah, Goodwin?" he growled

"I have information for you," I told him, "but first I would appreciate an answer to one question. Have you got tails tonight on any of the suspects in the Eads case?"

"Who wants to know?"

"All right, skip it. Get this quick. There were ten people at our place tonight. The five from Softdown—Helmar, Brucker, Quest, Pitkin, and Miss Duday. Also Sarah Jaffee and her attorney, Parker. Also Eric Hagh—the ex-husband. He flew in to-day—"

"I know he did."

"Hagh and his lawyer, Irby. Also Andy Fomos. They left a little after midnight. Sometime during the evening one of them took the keys to Sarah Jaffee's apartment out of her bag. She didn't miss them until she got home, and she phoned me, and I'm here now in her apartment. Whoever took her keys came and got in and waited for her, and at two minutes to two he conked her and strangled her, and she's dead. She's here on the floor. I'm telling it like this because it's now just two-thirty-six, and thirty-eight minutes isn't much time for getting out of this building and getting some-where, and if you get a move on—"

"Is this straight, Goodwin?"

"Yes."

"You're in the Jaffee apartment now?"

"Yes."

"By God, you stay there!"

"Drop that phone and get your hands up!"

It was a little confusing, with two city employees giving me commands at once, one on the phone and one in person but behind my back. Purley Stebbins had hung up, so that was all right. I turned, lifting my hands plenty high enough to show that they were empty, because there is no telling how a random flatfoot will act just after discovery of a corpse. He may have delusions of grandeur.

Evidently he was alone. He advanced, with his gun poked out, and it was no wonder if his hand was not perfectly steady, for it was a ticklish situation for a solitary cop, knowing as he did that I was armed. Probably he also knew of Sarah Jaffee's connection with Softdown and Priscilla Eads, since it had been in the papers, and if so why shouldn't I be the strangler the whole force was looking for and therefore good for a promotion and a barrel of glory, dead or alive?

"Look," I said, "I've just been talking to Sergeant Purley Stebbins of Manhattan—"

"Save it." He was dead serious. "Turn around, go to the wall, slow, put your palms up high against the wall, and keep 'em there."

I did as I was told. It was a routine arrangement for a solo frisk, and when I was in position I expected to feel the muzzle in my back and his hand going through me, but no. Instead, I heard him dialing the phone, and in a moment his voice. "This is Casey, gimme the lieutenant. . . . Lieutenant Gluck? Casey again. I came on up to the Jaffee apartment alone without waiting. I walked right in on him cold, and he's here, and I've got him covered. . . . No, I know that, but I've got him and I'll keep him until they come. . . ."

That was the kind of specimen, flushed by the hackie, who had me with my palms pressed against the wall.

During the eight-hour period from ten minutes to two Friday morning, when Sarah
Jaffee phoned me that her keys were missing, until nine o'clock Monday morning,
when I phoned Wolfe from the office of the
police commissioner, I had maybe five hours'
sleep, not more.

The first two hours of those eighty I spent
in the apartment of the late Sarah Jaffee,
mostly—after some grownups had arrived
and rescued me from Casey—seated at the
table in the alcove where I had breakfasted
with Sarah Wednesday morning, answering
questions put to me by a captain named
Olmstead from Manhattan Homicide West,
who was a comparative stranger. The third
strangling of course had the whole department sizzling, and the scientists had a high
old time that night in that apartment. The
murderer's use of the bronze tiger bookend
and the cord, which had been cut from a
venetian blind in the alcove, showed that he
had not confined his movements to the foyer,
and there wasn't a square inch anywhere in
the place that didn't get powdered for prints

and inspected with a glass under a strong light.

At 4:30 A.M. I was transported to the Nineteenth Precinct station on East Sixty-seventh Street, put into an upstairs room with a lieutenant and another dick with a stack of stenographer's notebooks, and told to give a complete account of the meeting in Wolfe's office, including all words and actions of everyone there. That took four hours, and during the fourth and last the three of us disposed of a dozen ham sandwiches, six muskmelons, and a gallon of coffee, paid for by me. When it was over I got permission to use a phone and called Wolfe.

"I'm calling from a desk phone in a police station," I told him, "and a lieutenant is at my elbow and a sergeant is on an extension, so don't say anything incriminating. I am not under arrest, though I am technically guilty of breaking and entering because I knocked the glass out of a door and went in. Except for that I have nothing to report, and I don't know when I'll be home. I have given them a complete account of last night in our office, and they'll certainly be after you for one."

"They already have been. Lieutenant

Rowcliff will be here at eleven o'clock, and I have agreed to admit him. Have you had breakfast?"

He wouldn't overlook that. I told him yes.

After that the lieutenant and sergeant left me, and I sat for a solid hour in a room with a uniformed patrolman. It began to look as if history was getting set to repeat itself, except for handcuffs, when a dick entered and told me to come on, and I preceded him down and out to the sidewalk, and darned if he didn't have a taxi waiting. It took us to 155 Leonard Street, and the dick took me in and upstairs to a room, and who should enter to visit me but my friend Mandelbaum, the assistant DA who had chatted with me Tuesday afternoon to no avail.

Four hours later we were still, as far as I could see, short on avail. I had the highly unsatisfactory feeling that I had been examined down to the last flick about something that had happened somewhere sometime, just to see if I passed, but that it had nothing to do with getting the sonofabitch I was after. I knew how to be patient well enough when I had to be, and I had gone along the best I could, but more than twelve hours had passed since I had opened the door and seen her lying there with her tongue sticking out, and I had answered enough questions.

At the end of the four hours Mandelbaum shoved his chair back, got up, and told me, "That seems to be it for now. I'll get it typed, and I'll get a copy of your statement uptown. This evening or in the morning—more likely in the morning—I'll ring you to ask you to run down and look it over, so stay near your phone or keep in touch."

I was frowning at him. "You mean I go?"

"Certainly. Under the circumstances your forceful entry to that building must be regarded as justified, and since you have agreed to pay the amount of the damage, there will be no complaint. Stay in the jurisdiction, of course, and be available." He looked at his wrist. "There's someone waiting for me." He turned to go.

I was having an experience that was not new to me. I had suddenly discovered that a decision had been made, by me, upon full consideration, without my knowing it. This time, though, it took me a second to accept it, because it was unprecedented. An officer of the law was telling me to go on home to

Nero Wolfe, and I didn't want to or intend to.

"Hold it," I said urgently, and he stopped. I appealed to him. "I've given you all I've got. I want something—not much. I want to see Inspector Cramer, and now. He's busy, and I don't know where he is, and it might take me until tomorrow to get to him. You fix it for me."

He was alert. "Is it about this case?"

"Yes."

"Why won't I do?"

"Because he can say yes to this, and you can't."

He might have been disposed to debate it if he hadn't been late for another customer. He glanced at his wrist again, went to the phone, and got busy. Even for him, the assistant DA on the Eads and Fomos case, it proved to be a job, but after ten minutes on the phone he told me, "He's in a conference at the Commissioner's office. Go there and send your name in and wait."

I thanked him as he rushed out.

I had had no lunch, and on the way to Centre Street, which wasn't much of a walk, I bought four nice ripe bananas and took them to a soda fountain and washed them down with a pint of milk.

At the office of Police Commissioner Skinner things did not look too promising. Not because there was an assortment of citizens in the large and busy anteroom, which was only normal, but because I couldn't find out who Mandelbaum had spoken to and I couldn't even get anyone to admit that Cramer was within. The trouble was that there was another door out of Skinner's office, around a corner of the corridor, and covering them both wasn't easy. However, I tried. I went outside and to the corner of the corridor—and there, standing by the other door, was Sergeant Purley Stebbins. At sight of me he started growling automatically.

I went up to him. "When did I ever ask you for a favor?"

"Never." He was hoarse, but he always was. "You're not that dumb."

"Not until now. I'm going to jump Inspector Cramer when he comes out, and ask him for five minutes, and you will kindly keep your trap shut. You can spoil it if you want to, but why should you want to? I'm a citizen, I pay taxes, and I've only been in jail nine times."

"He's busy."

"So am I."

"What do you want to ask him?"

I had the reply ready but didn't get to use it. The door opened, and Cramer came through and was with us. He was going to move right on, so preoccupied that he didn't even see me, until I stepped to cut him off.

"You?" He didn't like it. He darted a glance at Purley. "What's this?"

I got in. "My idea, Inspector. I've got something to say. If there's a room nearby we can use, five minutes ought to do it."

"I haven't got time."

"Make it four minutes."

He was scowling. "Wolfe sent you."

"No. *My* idea."

"What is it? Right here will do."

He moved to the wall, and I faced him. Purley made it a triangle. "At the DA's office," I said, "they told me to go on home. Instead, I came here to find you. You heard Mr. Wolfe there Tuesday, saying that I was his client. That was a swell gag, but also he more or less meant it—enough so that he sent me out to see if I could start some fur flying, and with luck I did, and last night they all came—"

"I know all about that."

"Okay. I felt some responsibility about Priscilla Eads. I grant it was only bad luck

241

that my using her for a stunt ended like that, but naturally I wanted to put a hand on the bastard that arranged the ending—"

"I know about that too. Get to it."

"I'm getting. This Sarah Jaffee is something else. It wasn't just bad luck. While she was telling me on the phone about her keys being gone, he was there in the closet waiting for her. I undertook to tell her what to do. Thinking that there was maybe one chance in a hundred that he was somewhere in the apartment—not more than that because I didn't know any reason for anyone wanting her dead, and I still don't—I told her what to do. I could have told her to run to an open window and start screaming, and that might have saved her. Or I could have told her to grab something to fight with—there was a stool right there at the phone—and back up to a wall and start yelling and pounding on the wall until someone came. But I didn't. I had something better. I didn't want to put him to the trouble of sneaking up on her, so I told her to go to him. I told her to go to the foyer and cross to the outside door, because that would take her within a few feet of the closet where he was hiding, and as he heard her approaching and passing, he could swing the door and take just one step, and wham. I told her just how to do it, and she followed instructions, though she had admitted to me that she was a coward. Hell, that wasn't just luck."

"What do you want, a medal?" Cramer rasped.

"No, thanks. I want a chance to touch him. Feeling as I do, I will not go home and sit on my ass while waiting for Mr. Wolfe to have a fit of genius, and go to bed at bedtime. It happens that I can help, and I would like to. For instance, of course everyone who was there last night has been questioned, but you won't finish with them until and unless it has been cracked. It was at Mr. Wolfe's office last night that her keys were taken. That must have been while my back was turned, because I have good eyes and I was using them last night. If one of them is being questioned now, I suggest that I be allowed to sit in and to offer comments if and when my memory says that one is needed, and that we go on that way until you get him. I claim to be qualified by the fact that I was present last night, with my eyes open, and I know more about when the keys could have been taken and when they couldn't than anybody could learn in a month of questioning. Also I will be glad to help in any other way that may be useful, except that I will not take Lieutenant Rowcliff's hand to lead him across the street."

He grunted. "A typical Wolfe approach."

"No. My one talk with Mr. Wolfe was at nine this morning with a lieutenant standing by and a sergeant listening in. This is strictly personal, as described, purely because I don't expect to feel like sleeping for a while."

He went to Purley. "He was there, and he could help. You know him as well as I do. What about it? Is this straight?"

"It's possible," the sergeant granted. "His head's been swelling a long time now, and it got a bad jolt, and he can't stand it. I'd buy it. We can always toss him out."

Cramer came to me. "If this is a dodge, I'll hook you good. Nothing goes to Wolfe, not a damn word, and nothing to the press or anyone else."

"Right."

"This was already a big noise, as you know, and now with this third one, another strangling, everybody in town has joined in. Two dozen copies have been made of your full report, and the Commissioner himself is studying one of them right now. Deputy Commissioner Wade is in a room down the hall with Brucker. At the DA's, Bowen is with Miss Duday, and Mandelbaum was to start again on Hagh, the ex-husband, when he finished with you. You can join any one of them, and I'll phone that you're coming, or you can come with Stebbins and me. We're going to do a retake with Helmar."

"I'll go with you for a starter."

"Come on." He moved.

My first appearance as an informal adjunct of the NYPD, seated at the left of Inspector Cramer as he interviewed Perry Helmar, lasted for five hours. It was by no means the first time I had seen and heard Cramer perform, but the circumstances were new, because I was all for him with no reservations. As a spectator at a quiz job I am probably as hard to please as anybody around, after the countless times I have watched Wolfe work, and I thought Cramer was good with Helmar. He couldn't have read my report more than once, with the full day he had had, but his picture of the meeting at Wolfe's office was clear and accurate. I made no great contribution to the performance, supplying a few interpositions and a couple of suggestions, none of which made a noticeable whoosh. At nine o'clock Helmar was sent home without escort, after being told that he would probably be wanted again in the morning.

Cramer went off to another conference in the Commissioner's office, and Purley and I left the building together. He had been on duty thirteen hours, and his program was eat and sleep, and I offered to buy him fried clams at Louie's.

I don't know how I had learned that offering Purley fried clams at Louie's was like dangling a bit of red flannel in front of a bullfrog, since our intimacy, not social to begin with, had never reached the peak of a joint meal. In view of my new though temporary status with the NYPD, he hesitated only four or five seconds.

At Louie's I insisted on his company to a phone booth, and, with the door open and him at my elbow, I dialed and got Wolfe.

I apologized. "I should have called earlier to say I couldn't make it for dinner, but I was tied up. I was with Inspector Cramer and Sergeant Stebbins, questioning Perry Helmar. Cramer's idea is that since I was there at the meeting last night it may help for me to sit in, and I agree. I am now going to buy Sergeant Stebbins some seafood, and afterward, as an aid to digestion, I'm going to the DA's office and check in at a session with Andy Fomos—either that or one with Oliver Pitkin. So again I can't say when I'll be home. This triple homicide is of course a round-the-clock operation for the cops, and I might as well keep going until I drop—chasing the picturesque and the passionate, according to plan. I'll give you a ring someday."

There was a little noise like a chopped-off chuckle, which seemed ill timed. "The confounded doorbell keeps ringing," he complained. "But Fritz and I will manage. Keep me informed at your convenience."

It clicked in my ear. I hung up, slow motion, and sat for a moment. He was being picturesque himself. Either he intended to dig in and work on it, in which case he should have insisted on my coming home immediately to help, or he did not intend to, in which case he should have beefed about my fraternizing with our ancient enemies.

"You know," I told Purley, "eccentrics are such interesting people."

"Not to me," he objected. "Every goddam murderer I've ever seen was an eccentric."

By the time he had finished two full portions of fried clams with trimmings, two steins of ale, and two pieces of apple pie

247

with cheese, I was fairly well caught up on the routine aspects. There had been no tails on any of them Thursday night, including Andy Fomos. Within five minutes after getting my phone call Purley had started twenty men checking on them, some by phone and some in person, covering everyone who had been at the meeting at Wolfe's office, not excluding Nathaniel Parker. Though four of them, including Parker, apparently had alibis—still being investigated—no one was conclusively eliminated, and no one was conclusively indicated.

On that Purley had a comment. When I got the phone call from Sarah Jaffee, if I had called Purley at once, and if he had jumped on it and had not only sent a man to Eightieth Street but had also immediately started the check on all concerned, we would now have the strangler. I agreed—but, I asked, if I had called him at once, would he have jumped on it; and he had to admit he wouldn't, chiefly because there was no known motive for any of them to kill Sarah Jaffee. Even if I had told him about the threat of Sarah's applying for an injunction, it would be stretching it thin to suppose one of them would murder her for that.

As for the alibis, whether they stood up

or not, the law felt the same as Wolfe when he told Viola Duday that while she might not have committed the crimes there was no reason why she shouldn't have contrived them. Purley said they had twenty-six men, the ones best qualified for that chore, trying to find a connection between one of the suspects and a death jobber. It was simpler in a way, but also harder in a way, because they were after a strangler, not a gunman.

They hadn't found a hackie who had taken a fare, between midnight and 1:45, to the address on East Eightieth or the immediate neighborhood, or from there after two o'clock. They were still looking, but the chances were slim. There was a subway station only three blocks away.

The name of the night man was William Fisler. My appraisal had been sound; he was a dope. At first he had maintained that from 12:30 to 1:45, the period during which the murderer must have got in and up to the apartment, he had been right on the job every minute, on guard near the front entrance, except for a couple of elevator trips with known tenants; but when he realized that if he stuck to that he was allowing the murderer, for entry to the building and the stairs, only the times of the brief elevator trips, he did a full flop and practically stated that he had been so busy downstairs with sandwiches and coffee that he had hardly seen the front entrance at all. His position was approximately the same for the period from 1:58 to 2:23, during which the murderer must have descended the stairs and made his exit to the sidewalk, and on away. He did admit that around a quarter to two he had been out on the sidewalk with the door to the building standing open, because he had to; Sarah's statement to me on the phone that that had been the situation when she and Parker arrived in a taxi had been corroborated by Parker.

Parker's alibi was airtight. Sarah had told me that he had not entered the building with her; the night man verified it; and the taxi driver, who of course had been found, and who had taken Parker on home, had testified likewise.

The murder itself presented no problem. Having got himself in, the murderer had selected the bronze tiger and the venetian blind cord as the proper tools, and concealed himself in the closet. If his plan had been to attack her at once when she entered, he had been forced to abandon it by the fact that the night man was there, letting her in. She had gone at once to the phone in the living room to call me, and of course that was no place for an act of violence, by a phone with the line open. When he heard her steps coming to the foyer, either he didn't know she had left the line open, or he couldn't resist so near a target, or he was afraid she was going outside; anyway, he struck. That done, he left, took the stairs down, and either found the main hall deserted and went out that way, or continued down to the basement and departed by the service alley.

No fingerprints found in the apartment had been those of any of the suspects. There had been none on the bronze tiger, and none on the knob of the closet door.

They were hunting a motive. Whereas with Priscilla Eads the motive had been as plain as the nose on a face, and fitted all five faces, with Sarah Jaffee there was none at all. For one of them to kill her, or have her killed, on account of the threatened injunction would have been batty, and none of those five was anywhere near batty. So finding a motive for any one of them would have been a big help, and that was a major objective of the supplementary questioning. Two of the five hours Cramer had spent with Helmar, me present, had been devoted to a thorough and fine-tooth review of his association with Sarah Jaffee from the beginning to the end.

Purley unquestionably briefed me. It didn't look as if he was holding anything back, and I was touched. Therefore, when the waiter brought the check and he insisted on splitting it, and during the debate he made a crack about city dicks not starving, I made it a point of honor because I got what was eating him. He knew that my take-home pay, considering that my home was with Wolfe, was at least four times his, and he wasn't going to sponge fried clams off of any goddam plutocrat. So I had to tell him I had invited him and my honor was at stake.

We parted outside, him going west and me heading for Leonard Street. I had my pick of Fomos or Pitkin, and on the way I voted for Pitkin.

—15—

At five o'clock Saturday morning I sat in a room at Leonard Street, reading papers from a folder. Pitkin had been sent home half an hour previously, from another room. This was the room where all reports and documents bearing on the three stranglings, either originals or copies, were being collected and held, and the report I was reading was about the movements of Jay Brucker during the rest of Thursday night after he left the meeting at Wolfe's office. The correctness of some of his statements seemed to be in question, and I was trying to find a basis of an opinion on whether, instead of going home to Brooklyn as he claimed, he had actually gone to Sarah Jaffee's apartment on Eightieth Street or to Daphne O'Neil's apartment on Fourth Street.

A voice said, "Hey, Goodwin, better knock off."

An assistant DA and two clerks were in the room, sorting and arranging the papers and folders, and the voice was the assistant DA's. I yanked myself up. I had been two-thirds asleep. It was silly to pretend I could sit there and read.

"There's a room down the hall with a couch," one of them said, "and no one will be in it today. It's Saturday."

I would have given a million dollars to be on a couch, so I decided against it. I arose, announced that I was going for a walk and would be back before long, and beat it.

Emerging from the building to the sidewalk, I got a shock—it was daylight. Dawn had come, and that helped to wake me and changed my outlook. I stood at the curb, and when a taxi loomed before long, headed uptown, I flagged it and gave the driver the address I knew best.

At that time of day we had Manhattan all to ourselves. West Thirty-fifth was empty too as I paid the hackie and climbed out. Since the chain bolt would of course be on the front door, instead of mounting the stoop I went down the four steps to the area door and pushed the button. It buzzed in the kitchen and Fritz's room. There were sounds from within, a door opening and footsteps, and Fritz gave me a look through the peep-glass and then opened up.

"Good God," he said, "you look awful."

I told him that was precisely why I had dropped in, to remedy that condition, apologized for disturbing him, and proceeded upstairs. Without even a glance in at the office as I passed by, I went on up to my room and started in on a shower, a shave, and a complete change. When I had finished I may or may not have looked better, but I sure felt better. Descending to the ground floor, I heard sounds in the kitchen and went in. Fritz was there, putting on his apron.

"What now?" I demanded. "It's only half-past six."

"Orange juice in two minutes. Breakfast in ten—enough to start."

"I'm on my way out."

"You'll eat first."

So I did, though I felt that it was bad manners to eat Wolfe's grub under the circumstances. Fritz kept me company, sitting on a stool and yawning while he wasn't serving the meal. At one point he observed, "This is getting to be a habit."

"What is?"

"This early breakfast. Yesterday about this time—a little later—I was poaching eggs for Mr. Wolfe and Saul."

I stopped a bite of pancake in midair. "You were what?"

"Poaching eggs for Mr. Wolfe and Saul."

I put the bite where it belonged and chewed slowly. Saul Panzer looked less, and acted more, like the best all-around operative in New York than any other candidate I had ever seen or heard of. He was so good that he could free-lance without an office and make more than anyone on a payroll. He was always Wolfe's first choice when we had to have help, and we had used him hundreds of times.

I asked casually, "Saul's taking over my job, I suppose?"

"I don't know," Fritz said firmly, "anything about what Saul is doing."

That was plain enough. Obviously Fritz had been told that if I came around it was okay for me to know that Saul had come to an early breakfast, but no more. I made no effort to snake it out of him, having tried it once or twice before with no success at all.

On my way out I stopped in the office. Friday's mail, under a paperweight on Wolfe's desk, contained nothing that couldn't wait. There was nothing on the desk, or on the memo pad or calendar, that gave any hint of what he wanted with Saul, but in the safe I found something that indicated that it was no trivial chore. I opened the safe because I wanted to hit petty cash for a loan. One of the drawers of the safe is partitioned in the middle, with petty cash on the right and emergency reserve on the left. Getting five twenties from petty, I noticed a slip of paper in emergency that hadn't been there before, and I picked it up for a look. Scribbled on it in pencil in Wolfe's neat hand was the notation, "6/27/52 $2000

NW." It was the long-standing rule to keep five grand in emergency, in used hundreds, twenties, and tens. A quick count showed that the slip was a record of a real transaction; two grand had been taken. That was interesting—so darned interesting that I might have forgotten to tell Fritz so long if he hadn't heard me leaving the office and come out to put the bolt back on the door. I told him it was okay to let Wolfe know I had been in for an early breakfast, but no more.

Returning to Leonard Street in a taxi, naturally I tried to decide what Saul Panzer was supposed to be doing with two thousand bucks, granting that it was in connection with Eads-Fomos-Jaffee. I concocted quite a list of guesses, beginning with a trip to Venezuela to check on Eric Hagh, and ending with a bribe to Andy Fomos to spill something his wife had told him. I bought none of them.

The five hours' sleep that I mentioned getting between early Friday morning and Monday morning came Sunday from four a.m. to 9 a.m., on a bumpy old couch at the headquarters of Manhattan Homicide West on Twentieth Street. I might be able, by digging hard, to give a complete report and timetable of a hundred other activities I had a share in during that stretch, but I don't know what good it would do you, and if you don't mind I would rather skip it. I sat in at a couple of dozen quiz sessions, at Twentieth Street, Leonard Street, and Centre Street. I read tens of thousands of words of reports and summaries. Most of Sunday I spent in a PD car with a uniformed driver, with credentials signed by a deputy commissioner, calling on a long list of people who were connected in one way or another with something that had been said by one of the suspects. Returning to Twentieth Street Sunday around midnight, I admit I had in mind the possibility of another date with the couch, but I didn't get it. Brucker's alibi had been cracked. Feeling hot breath just behind him, he was now claiming that he had gone from Wolfe's house to Daphne O'Neil's apartment and spent the night there, and she was concurring. When I got in from my Sunday drive, Captain Olmstead was just starting to take Daphne over the bumps, and I was invited to join the party, and accepted. It ended around six a.m. Monday, and my thoughts again dived for the couch, but I didn't. I had to either get a clean shirt or go off and hide, so I went to Thirty-fifth Street and repeated Saturday's performance, including a breakfast by Fritz.

Of course I didn't see Wolfe. I had phoned him once each day, but no mention had been made of murder or Saul Panzer. He was testy, and I was touchy. I looked in the safe again; no more dough had been taken from emergency.

Returning to Twentieth Street, superficially clean and fresh, but pretty well fagged, and no bargain even at half price, I was going along the upper hall when one of my colleagues—for I might as well face it and admit it, during that period Homicide dicks were my colleagues—coming out of a room, caught sight of me, and yelled, "Hey, where the hell have you been?"

"Look at me." I pointed to my shirt and tie. "Doesn't it show?"

"Yeah, let me touch you. I was going to send out a general alarm. They want you down at the Commissioner's office."

"Who wants me?"

"Stebbins phoned twice. He's there with the inspector. There's a car down front. Come on."

Some chauffeurs of PD cars like to have an excuse to step on it, and some don't.

That one did. He didn't use much noise, but plenty of gas, and when he was in the fourth grade a maladjusted schoolteacher had made him write five hundred times, "A miss is as good as a mile," and it sank in. I should have clocked us from 230 West Twentieth Street to 240 Centre Street. As I got out I told him he should have an insurance vending machine, like those at airports, installed on his dash, and he grinned sociably. "Impressed you, did it, bud?"

It did, at that, but not as much as the assortment I found waiting for me in the spacious and well-furnished office of Police Commissioner Skinner. Besides Skinner and District Attorney Bowen, there were two deputy commissioners, Cramer and another inspector, a deputy inspector, a captain, and Sergeant Purley Stebbins—and they were certainly waiting for me, from the way all faces turned and stayed turned as I entered and advanced.

Skinner told me to sit, and they had a chair waiting too. He asked Bowen, "You want to take it, Ed?"

"No, go ahead," the DA told him.

Skinner eyed me. "I guess you know as much about where we stand as I do."

I lifted my shoulders and let them down.

"I don't know about the rest of you, but I'm flat on my back."

He nodded. "We all are, not for quotation. Most of us gave up our weekends, but we might as well not have. During the last forty hours we've had more men on this case than any other in my time, and I can't see that we've gained an inch, and the others agree with me. It is an extremely bad situation, it couldn't be worse, and something has to be done. We've been discussing it here at length, and various proposals have been made and some adopted, and one of them concerns you. We want your help on it."

"I've been trying to help."

"I know you have. Ever since I read your report last Friday I have thought that our best single chance was the keys. Those keys were lifted from a lady's bag while twelve people were present in the room. I don't think it's possible that no one saw any significant glance or movement. As you know, they have been questioned over and over, and the only result has been to focus suspicion on Hagh, the ex-husband, because he was nearer Mrs. Jaffee than anyone else for most of the evening. But all of them had opportunities, as you make clear in your report—and in fact they don't deny it. We certainly can't charge Hagh just because he had more chances than the rest of them; and, besides that, what was his motive, and where would that leave us on the first two murders? Do you argue with that?"

"No, I've got no arguments left."

"And arguments don't catch murderers anyway. I agree. We want to make an all-out effort to get a line on the lifting of the keys. More questions won't do it. We want to take them to Nero Wolfe's office and have them go through it, with Wolfe and you taking part, of course. Words and actions. We want them to repeat, as closely as they can, everything they said and did Thursday evening, with three or four of us present, and we want to take a tape recording of it."

I lifted my brows at him.

"Mostly," he said, "to try to spot who took the keys, but there's another thing. If someone wanted to kill Mrs. Jaffee, why did he wait until then to do it? Why didn't he kill her before? Was it because he had no motive before? Was it something that happened that evening that gave him the motive? We want to watch for that too. We haven't found it in any of the reports or statements, but we might possibly get it this way. We want to try, and we'll have to have Wolfe's and your cooperation. We can't compel him to let us in his place with them, much less compel him to do his part. We want you to phone him or go to see him, whichever you think is better, and make the request of him."

"I want to say, Goodwin," the DA put in, "that I regard it as extremely important that this be done. It *must* be done."

"You guys," I said emphatically, "have one hell of a nerve."

"Come on," Cramer rasped, "don't start that hard-to-get stuff, and don't be witty."

"Poops." I took them in. "Last Tuesday, six days ago, I sat on a bench in this building with handcuffs on. You may remember also that Mr. Wolfe was conveyed to Leonard Street under a warrant, and you know how he felt about that. Wanting to make a scene, he announced that I was his client, and he was stuck. He had to go through some motions, and he did; and, acting for him, I pulled Sarah Jaffee in, and she got it. That threw me off balance, and I made a mistake. I asked to work with you because I thought that way I would be in it more, and I guess I have been, but where are we? And Mr. Wolfe is sore as a pup, and you know damn well he is, and yet you have the gall to ask me to ask him this, because you think if you ask him he'll say no. I think so too, but I also think he'll say no if I ask him. Take your pick—would you rather have him say no to you or to me?"

"We want him to say yes," Skinner declared.

"So do I, but I don't think there's a glimmer. Do you want me to try?"

"Yes."

"When do you want to stage it? Today?"

"As soon as possible. We can have them there in half an hour."

I looked at my wrist; it was ten to nine. I might catch him before he went up to the plant rooms. "Which phone do I use?"

Skinner indicated one of the five on his desk, even going so far as to lift the receiver and hand it to me as I stepped over. I gave the number and soon had Wolfe's voice.

"Archie. Have you finished breakfast?"

"Yes." He didn't sound so peevish. I knew him so well, and all the thousand shades and keys of his voice, that one "yes" gave me the tune. He added, "Fritz tells me you had yours here."

"Yeah, I needed to rinse off. I'm calling

264

you at the request of the People of the State of New York."

"Indeed."

"As represented by quite a mixture—the Police Commissioner and two of his deputies, the District Attorney, a bunch of inspectors and deputy inspectors, not to mention Sergeant Purley Stebbins. I'm talking from the private office of the Commissioner—you know it; you've been here. After these days and nights of camaraderie with them—is that the way to pronounce it?"

"Almost."

"Good. I am held in high esteem by the whole shebang, from Commissioner all the way down to Lieutenant Rowcliff, which is quite a distance. Wanting to show me what they think of me, they are bestowing a great honor on me. Having a request to make of you, they are letting me make it. They're all sitting here gazing at me so tenderly I've got a lump in my throat. You ought to see them."

"How long are you going to drag this out?"

"I'm through dragging. Here's the point. We're flumped. We have got to try something different—like this, for instance. We want to do a playback of the session at the office Thursday evening, with the original cast, and take a tape recording of it. We'll bring the personnel, with the exception of Sarah Jaffee, and the recorder, and all you will have to do is let us in and play your part. I have told my associates, who have done me the favor of letting me make this phone call, that I am practically certain you will tell us to go to hell; and since nothing gives you more pleasure than to prove me wrong, here's a chance for some good clean fun. All you have to do—"

"Archie."

"Yes, sir."

"When do you want to do this?"

"Today. As soon as possible. Of course you won't be down from the plant rooms until eleven—"

"Very well." He was gruff but not wroth. "As you know, I have stated before witnesses that you are my client in this instance, and I never refuse a reasonable request from a client. This request seems reasonable. Therefore I grant it."

It was unexpected, no doubt about that, but my chief reaction was not surprise. It was surmise. His noble sentiment about humoring his client, especially when I was it, was pure guff. Something else was moving him, and what?

He was going on. "However, eleven will be too early, as I'll be engaged. Shall we say twelve o'clock? Will that be convenient?"

"Yes, sir, that will suit fine. I'll come on up pretty soon and get things arranged, chairs and so on."

"No." He was emphatic. "You will not. Fritz and I can manage. Your associates in the Police Department need you more than I do. Be here at twelve." He hung up.

I cradled the phone and told my audience, "Mr. Wolfe says okay. We're to be there at noon."

I didn't add that I had a strong suspicion there were going to be some script revisions, not by any of us and not by any of the cast.

—16—

The idea, I don't know whose, was to go in a body, after gathering at the Tenth Precinct station, and it was quite a cavalcade, with two limousines—Skinner's and Bowen's—and four PD sedans.

I was in Skinner's limousine, and at my suggestion it headed the procession. I thought I should be the first to enter, and intended, on crossing the threshold, to change over and become a host, but discovered that it had been planned differently. It was not Fritz who let us in, but Saul Panzer, and he greeted me as an arriving guest, offering to take my hat. He could kid me, and often did, but not in the presence of the Police Commissioner. Wolfe had told him to, no question about it. So I said, "Thank you, sonny," and handed him the hat, and he said, "Don't mention it, officer."

Wolfe and Fritz, with Saul's help evidently, had managed well enough. The chairs were placed exactly as they had been at the start of the proceedings Thursday evening, and the portable bar was at its spot, fully equipped. There was some displacement when Purley and a dick came with the tape recorder and accessories and got it installed, but things were properly rearranged. Since I was being regarded as a guest I thought it was only polite to act like one, so I went to my desk and sat, which was where I belonged as a member of the cast. The other members likewise disposed themselves, and none of them needed any coaching. Nearest me was Viola Duday, then Oliver Pitkin, Jay Brucker, and Bernard

Quest, and Perry Helmar in the red leather chair. The couch, to my right and rear as I faced Wolfe's desk, was not occupied. Sarah Jaffee had sat there Thursday. On a chair near it was Eric Hagh, and beyond him were the two lawyers, Irby and Parker. Andy Fomos was off by himself, over by the bookshelves.

Additional chairs, some of the smaller yellow ones, had been lined up along the wall on the other side of Wolfe's desk, for the audience. It seemed bad etiquette for VIPs like the Police Commissioner and the District Attorney and Inspector Cramer to be perched on those skimpy little numbers while Helmar, a mere Wall Street lawyer and murder suspect, had the red leather chair all to himself, but the occasion required it. Also in the row of audience were Assistant DA Mandelbaum, Captain Olmstead, and Purley Stebbins. The recorder was on a table at Purley's elbow.

Saul Panzer stood facing the cast, not the audience. There is nothing impressive about Saul. He is undersized, his nose and ears are too big, and his shoulders slant. With Saul a thousand wrongdoers had made the mistake of believing what they saw. He spoke. "I believe this is the way it was Thursday evening when Mr. Wolfe entered. Does any-one disagree?"

No one did. He went on, "I'll sit on the couch where Mrs. Jaffee was. I wasn't here, but it has been described to me, and if I do anything wrong it can be corrected. Archie, will you ring for Mr. Wolfe as you did Thursday?"

He passed between Viola Duday and me to get to the couch. I stepped to Wolfe's desk and pressed the button, one long and two short, and returned to my chair. Wolfe entered. On account of the row of audience he couldn't bear right along the wall, so he navigated through the cast to make his desk. Standing beside his chair, he took his time for a look from right to left, ending with those against the wall, the representatives of the People of the State of New York.

"You gentlemen don't look very comfort-able," he muttered.

They said they were all right. He sat. There was a tingle in my spine. I knew his look and manner as well as I did his voice, and there was no doubt about it, he was going to pull one, or try to.

He addressed the District Attorney. "I assume, Mr. Bowen, that these people know why you have brought them here?"

Bowen nodded. "Yes, it's been thoroughly explained to them, and they have all agreed to cooperate. Mr. Helmar, Mr. Parker, and Mr. Irby have made certain reservations about the use of the recording, and they have been covered in a memo. Do you want to see it?"

"Not if Mr. Parker has approved it. Then we may proceed?"

"Please do."

Wolfe turned. "Miss Duday and gentlemen. You understand that the purpose of this gathering is for us to iterate our words and movements of last Thursday evening. The first thing that happened after I entered the room was Mr. Goodwin's identification for me of Miss Duday and Messrs. Brucker, Quest, and Pitkin. Then I sat down. Then Mr. Helmar said he had a statement he would like to read, and that, I suppose, is where we should start, but before we do so I wish to make some remarks."

A sound came from one person, not one of the cast. It was Inspector Cramer, and the sound was a cross between a growl and a snort. Cramer knew Wolfe better than anyone there except me.

Wolfe leaned back and got comfortable. "I told you Thursday evening that my sole interest was investigation of the murder of Priscilla Eads, and that is still true, except that now the murder of Sarah Jaffee is joined to it. After you people left that evening I told Mr. Goodwin that I thought I knew who killed Miss Eads and Mrs. Fomos. That surmise, for that is all it was then, was based on two things: first, the impression I had got of you five people that evening; and second, the fact that Mrs. Fomos had been killed.

"The supposition that the attack on Mrs. Fomos was solely for the purpose of getting the keys to Miss Eads' apartment was clearly not acceptable if any alternative could be had. If that was all that was wanted it would only have been necessary to snatch her bag. A dozen women's bags are snatched every day in this city. Killing Mrs. Fomos greatly increased the hazard of killing Miss Eads. If her body had been discovered sooner, as it might easily have been, and if that city detective—Auerbach, was it, Mr. Cramer?"

"Yes." Cramer's eyes were narrowed at him.

"If he had got his notion about the keys more promptly, he would have got to Miss Eads' apartment before her return and would have found the murderer ambushed there.

Surely the murderer was capable of calculating such a risk, and he would have not have killed Mrs. Fomos except under a strong impulsion. This objection of course occurred to the police, and I understand that they met it by assuming that in his attempt to get the bag from Mrs. Fomos her assailant was recognized and so was compelled to kill her. That assumption was not impossible, but it implied that the murderer was an egregious bungler, and I doubted it. I preferred to assume exactly the opposite—that Mrs. Fomos had been killed, not because she had recognized her attacker, but because he knew she couldn't recognize him."

"Is this for effect?" Skinner demanded. "Or do you think you're getting somewhere?"

"I am already somewhere," Wolfe retorted. "I've just told you who the murderer is."

Purley Stebbins stood up with his gun in his hand, his eyes on the cast, trying to keep them all in focus at once.

"Go on and spell it," Cramer growled.

"He wanted the keys, certainly," Wolfe conceded, "but he didn't have to kill Mrs. Fomos to get them. He killed her because she was herself a danger to him, as great a danger as Miss Eads. It would have done him no good to kill the one unless he killed the other. That was my hypothesis as early as Tuesday evening, but there were then too many alternatives, more easily tested, to give it priority. Wednesday Mr. Goodwin called on Mrs. Jaffee and Mr. Fomos, and late that afternoon Mr. Irby came and provided me with bait to get you people here. Thursday morning Mrs. Jaffee came, as the result of a brilliant maneuver by Mr. Goodwin the day before, and gave me much better bait than Mr. Irby had supplied, and, as you all know, I used it. But for that maneuver by Mr. Goodwin, Mrs. Jaffee would not have come to see me, and almost certainly she would be alive now. That seems to me much firmer ground for his feeling of responsibility for her death than her phone call to him Thursday night and its sequel. It is regrettable, but not surprising, that his feeling was so intense as to warp his mental processes and pervert his judgment. I did and do sympathize with him."

"Is this all necessary?" Bowen wanted to know.

"Perhaps not," Wolfe allowed, "but I'm exposing a murderer and claim a measure of indulgence. You must have expected to spend hours here. Am I tedious?"

"Go ahead."

"And Thursday afternoon Mr. Irby returned with his client, Mr. Hagh, who had flown from Venezuela. I no longer needed him or his client as bait for you, but I invited them to join us that evening, provided they came as observers and not participants. As you know, they were here. What is it, Archie?"

"I'll tend to me," I told him. I had left my chair and was moving. I won't say I had caught up with him, but at least I could see his dust, and I admit that I had also seen Saul Panzer, not with any flourish, take a gun from his pocket and rest it on his thigh. I did not display a gun. I merely circled around the end of the couch and stopped, and stood less than arm's length northwest of Eric Hagh's right shoulder. He didn't turn his head, but he knew I was there. His eyes were glued to Wolfe.

"Okay," I told Wolfe. "I'm not warped enough to break his neck. How come?"

Satisfied that I wasn't going to throw a tantrum, he returned to the Softdown quintet. "When you left here Thursday evening, I had nothing new about you with regard to the murder of Miss Eads, but it seemed more than ever doubtful, under my hypothesis, that a motive could be found for any of you to kill Mrs. Fomos. As I said, I told Mr. Goodwin that I thought I knew who had committed the murders, but I also told him that there was a contradiction that had to be solved, and for that purpose I asked him to have Mrs. Jaffee here at eleven o'clock the next morning."

He turned left. "What was the contradiction, Mr. Cramer?"

Cramer shook his head. "I'm not clear up with you. I suppose the point was that this Eric Hagh is not Hagh, he's a ringer, from what you said about him killing Mrs. Fomos because he knew she couldn't recognize him, but then where were you?"

"I was facing a contradiction."

"What?"

"You should know. Among the items furnished by me to Lieutenant Rowcliff on Friday was a carbon copy of a report, typed by Mr. Goodwin, of his conversation with Mrs. Jaffee on Wednesday at her apartment. Surely you have read it, and this is an excerpt from it. I quote: 'That was the last letter I ever got from Pris. The very last.

Maybe I still have it—I remember she enclosed a picture of him.'

"Mrs. Jaffee said that to Mr. Goodwin. It contradicted my hypothesis that the man calling himself Eric Hagh was an impostor; for if Mrs. Jaffee had seen a picture of Hagh, why didn't she denounce this man when she saw him here? It was to get an answer to that question that I asked Mr. Goodwin to have her here Friday morning."

"Why didn't you ask her then and there?"

"If that's a challenge, Mr. Cramer, I ignore it. If it's a request for information, the—"

"It is."

"Good. The circumstances were not favorable. My suspicion of Hagh had no support but a hypothesis, and I was not certain of the bona fides of Mrs. Jaffee herself. I wanted first to get an opinion from Mr. Goodwin and Mr. Parker, and Mrs. Jaffee was leaving with Mr. Parker. It was late at night, and I was tired. Of course I regret it. I regretted it only two hours after I had gone to bed, when I was awakened by the phone and Mr. Goodwin told me that Mrs. Jaffee had been murdered. Then, too late for her, I knew. I even got out of bed and sat in a chair, something I never do."

"This is being recorded, Wolfe," Bowen warned him. "You say you knew the identity of a murderer. Whom did you notify?"

"Pfui. That's childish, Mr. Bowen. I had no evidence. You have had every scrap of information I have had, and the services of Mr. Goodwin to boot, which is a great advantage when his head is on straight. I had started, remember, with pure hypothesis, in an effort to account for the murder of Mrs. Fomos as a preamble to the murder of Miss Eads. In fact, I had started with several different hypotheses, but by far the most attractive was this: that someone in Caracas had got hold of the document Miss Eads, then Mrs. Hagh, had signed, giving her husband a half interest in her property, and was impersonating Hagh to make the claim; that, deciding he would have to come to New York in person to press the claim, he had determined to get rid of the only two people who, because they knew Hagh, made his appearance here impossible; and that either he came here himself and killed them, or contrived it.

"It became more than hypothesis when Mrs. Jaffee was killed. The killer had got her keys from her bag here that evening, and, so far as was known, no one else, of those present, had the slightest motive for killing Mrs. Jaffee. And my contradiction was resolved. Mrs. Jaffee had realized that Eric Hagh was not the man whose picture had been sent her by her friend six years ago, but she had not denounced him because it was not in her character to do so. She had revealed her character with some clarity to Mr. Goodwin. She didn't like to get involved with anyone or anything. She had never gone to a stockholders' meeting of the corporation whose dividends were her only source of income. She came here Thursday to lend her name to a legal action only because she was under great obligation to Mr. Goodwin. No, she did not denounce the impostor, but indubitably she made him aware that she knew he was not Eric Hagh. She may have done so merely by the way she looked at him, or she may have asked him some naive and revealing question. In any case, he knew he was in deadly peril from her, and he acted quickly and audaciously—and with dexterity, taking her keys from her bag. No, he is not a bungler, but—"

A voice broke in. It was Dewdrop Irby, and his voice was good and loud, with no oil at all in it. "I want to state at this time, for the record, that I had no—"

"Shut up!" Cramer barked at him.

"But I want—"

"You'll get what you want. I'll deliver it personally."

Wolfe asked, "Shall I finish?"

"Yes."

"As I said, I got out of bed and sat in a chair. It took little consideration for me to conclude that my hypothesis had been violently, tragically, and completely validated. I did not phone your office, Mr. Cramer, because it is not my habit to make the police a gift, unasked, of the product of my brain, because I was personally concerned, and because I knew how badly Mr. Goodwin's self-esteem had been bruised and I thought he would be gratified if we, not you, got the murderer. I did phone not long after getting the news from Mr. Goodwin— though not to you—and at three o'clock in the morning succeeded in reaching a man in Caracas whom I know a little and can trust within reason. Five hours later he called me back to say that Eric Hagh was new to Caracas and apparently had no background there."

"I could have told you that," Cramer

grumbled. "He has been living at the Orinoco Hotel for two months."

"It's a pity I didn't ask you and save twenty dollars. While waiting for the report from Caracas, I had phoned Saul Panzer. He had come and eaten breakfast with me, and I had supplied him with money from my emergency cash reserve. From here he went to a newspaper office and got pictures of the man calling himself Eric Hagh, and from there he went to Idlewild Airport. At ten o'clock he boarded a plane for South America."

"Not for Caracas," Purley Stebbins objected. He was still standing with his gun in hand. "Not at ten o'clock."

"He didn't go to Caracas. He went to Cajamarca, Peru. The document signed by Priscilla Eads Hagh was written there. At Cajamarca he found people who had known Hagh, and two who also remembered Mrs. Hagh, and he learned, one, that Hagh was a professional gambler; two, that he had not been in Cajamarca for three years; and three, that the pictures he had with him were not of Hagh. He flew to Lima, engaged the interest of the police by a method not utterly unknown in our own city, and within twelve hours had collected enough items to phone me. The items included—you tell them, Saul. Briefly."

Saul gave his voice a little more volume than usual, because he wasn't facing the bulk of his audience. He had his eyes straight at Eric Hagh and had no intention of shifting them.

"They had all known Eric Hagh," he said. "Hagh had been a gambler working up and down the coast for years. As far as they knew he had been in the States only twice, once for a spell in Los Angeles and once in New Orleans, and from New Orleans he brought back a rich American bride. They all knew about the paper he had, signed by his wife, giving him half her property. Hagh had shown it around, bragging about it. He said it had been her idea to give it to him, but he was too proud a man to sponge on a woman and he was keeping it as a souvenir. They said he had meant it; he was like that. I couldn't ask him because he was dead. He had been caught in a snow slide in the mountains three months ago, on March nineteenth. Nobody knew what had happened to the document."

Saul cleared his throat. He's always a little husky. "The man I had pictures of, the man I'm looking at now—his name is

Siegfried Muecke. Twenty-six people in Lima recognized him from the pictures. He was first seen there about two years ago, and no one knows where he came from. He is also a professional gambler, and he went around a good deal with Hagh. He was with him in the mountains, working a tourist resort with him, when Hagh was killed by a snow slide. Nobody has seen Siegfried Muecke around Lima since Hagh's death. Do you want more details?"

"Not at present, Saul," Wolfe told him.

Purley Stebbins was moving. He passed in front of Helmar and between Brucker and Quest, and around me, and posted himself directly behind Siegfried Muecke, who was now fairly well seen to, with Saul at his left, Purley at his rear, and me at his right.

Wolfe was going on. "Mr. Muecke's preparations for his coup, crossing the Andes to Caracas so as to operate from a base where he and Mr. Hagh were both unknown, can of course be traced. At Caracas he selected a lawyer, with some care probably, and decided to present his claim in a letter—not to the former Mrs. Hagh, but to the trustee of the property, Mr. Helmar. At some point he also decided that effective pursuit of the claim would require his presence in New

York, and of course it would be fatal to his plans if either Miss Eads or Mrs. Fomos ever got a glimpse of him. There was only one way to solve that difficulty: they must die."

"But not until after June thirtieth," Bowen objected.

Wolfe nodded. "That's a point, certainly, but it's not inexplicable. Looking at his face, which apppears rigid in paralysis, I doubt if he'll explain for us, not now at least. I offer alternatives: some incident may have alarmed him and precipitated action, or he may not have known that if Miss Eads died before June thirtieth the Softdown stock, the bulk of her fortune, would go to others. I think the latter more likely, since he was offered, through Mr. Irby, a cash settlement of one hundred thousand dollars and wouldn't even discuss it.

"Another point should soon be clarified, whether Mr. Muecke is persuaded to help or not. Did he arrange for the murders of Miss Eads and Mrs. Fomos, or did he commit them himself? That can of course be established by inquiry in Caracas and of airline personnel. I think you'll find that he did them himself. You should be able to verify his first flight to New York, and surely you will have no trouble with his return to Caracas, since he must have left New York on Tuesday to be in Caracas to speak with Mr. Irby on the telephone on Wednesday. Also, he had to leave Caracas again Wednesday afternoon or evening to get back to New York Thursday, and we know he did that."

Wolfe's eyes fixed on Muecke, and he spoke to him for the first time. "For myself, Mr. Muecke, there is no room for doubt. You set your pattern and kept to it with pigheaded constancy. You waylaid Mrs. Jaffee, and struck and strangled her, exactly as you had done with Miss Eads, and previously with Mrs. Fomos. I said you were no bungler, but the truth is—Archie!"

I had noticed once before, when he had slammed the door in my face, that Andy Fomos could move fast when he wanted to. He was out of his chair and across the room to our little group like a flying saucer. Apparently his idea was to do something to Muecke with his bare hands, as his personal comment on what Muecke had done to Mrs. Fomos, but there was no time to analyze ideas, including my own. Now, at leisure, I can and I have, and to complete the record I report the results.

The question is, since the worst Andy Fomos could have done was to disfigure Muecke superficially, why did I want to interfere? Why didn't I give him gangway and even block Purley? Why did I haul off and plug Andy's iron jaw with so much behind it that he sailed through the air before he stretched out, and my wrist and knuckles were stiff for a week? The answer is, if I had touched Muecke I would have killed him, but I had to touch somebody or something, and Andy Fomos, bless his hundred and ninety pounds that made it really satisfactory, gave me the excuse.

Then Cramer was there, and Skinner, and I sidestepped to make room, and stood, licking blood from my knuckles and watching Purley get handcuffs on Siegfried Muecke.

The publishers hope that this
Large Print Book has brought
you pleasurable reading.
Each title is designed to make
the text as easy to see as possible.
G.K. Hall Large Print Books
are available from your library and
your local bookstore. Or, you can
receive information by mail on
upcoming and current Large Print Books
and order directly from the publishers.
Just send your name and address to:

G.K. Hall & Co.
70 Lincoln Street
Boston, Mass. 02111

or call, toll-free:

1-800-343-2806

A note on the text
Large print edition designed by
Kipling West.
Composed in 16 pt Plantin
on a Xyvision 300/Linotron 202N
by Stephen Traiger
of G.K. Hall & Co.